ODE TO AN OUTLAW

Vol. 2 of Stony Diamond The Texas Shooter

JACK R. STANLEY

Wrightbridge Press

Ode To An Outlaw
Copyright © 2020 by Jack R. Stanley
Wrightbridge Press
All rights reserved.
ISBN: 978-1-947726-98-7

This is a work of fiction. Any resemblance to any persons, events or localities is purely coincidental and beyond the intent of the author and publisher.

Credits:
Cover by
Courtney Stengel
Edited by
Mary Lee Stanley
and
Rose Marie Reed

jacks@wrightbridgepress.com
www.thefictionwritersnotebook.com
www.jackrstanley.com

DEDICATION

To the love of my life
Mary Lee
who makes all things possible.

CHAPTER 1

Jingle bobs are the cowboy's reward. They are a pair of solid cone-shaped steel dangles mounted in twos on each side of the center rod of a spurs' rowels. The adornments jingle with each step and announce the owner as a top hand. Ranch owners award them to their best riders, ropers, and overall cowhands.

Willet Hatcher had celebrated his new honor. But even at 22, he knew his limits and knew it was time to stop this celebration. Sunup was going to be there in only a few hours, and he would be back in the saddle and putting in a full day's work. He slammed his empty whisky glass down on the bar as his fellow riders tossed coins on the hard surface to cover the cost. Willet staggered a little but got himself upright and headed for the saloon's front door. He wobbled again and bumped a poker player before getting himself erect once more.

"Sorry, partner," he said, patting the cocky young player on the shoulder. "My fault. Didn't mean t' jossle ya.'" He walked on but got only two more steps before the card player jumped to his feet and slammed his chair back to the stuffed and worn wooden floor.

"You son-of-a-bitch!" the gambler shouted, stopping Willet with a challenge and causing the young hand to turn back from the door.

"I'm a little drunk," Willet slurred. "Celebrating my jingle bobs," he braced himself against the door and lifted one of his boots. "I'm sorry I bumped ya'. Didn't mean to. I need t' get me some sleep — and sober up."

"No, what you need to do is go for your hog leg! Nobody touches me 'less I allow 'em. I'm going to kill you, cowboy."

"What?" the short and muscular rider asked, believing he misheard the gunman's remark.

"I said, draw."

Willet shook his head to clear his mind. "Mister, I ain't no gun-hand."

"You're wearing a shooting iron. Use it!"

"This ol' thing," Willet said, glancing down at

his weapon. "It's for shootin' snakes — and horses that need t' be put out of their misery?"

"I'm going to put you out of your misery. Now, draw!"

The saloon was silent for a moment. Willet began breathing rapidly as another chair was heard being pushed away from a table.

"Go home, cowboy," a deep voice called out.

"Don't move!" the gunman said.

Willet didn't know what to do.

The next sound heard was of another pistol being cocked.

Once more, the voice said, "You did nothing wrong, cowboy. Certainly nothing worth dying for. You apologized — go home. Now!"

The gunman turned to find a tall man — 6 foot 1, with brown hair, wearing a black frock coat with matching vest and pants. His shirt was grey with a string tie. He also wore a grey Stetson. He held a cocked Smith and Wesson American .44 single-action revolver in his hand.

"You know who I am?" the card-playing gunman asked.

"Don't know — don't care," the man with the .44 said.

"Somebody bumps me — somebody's going to pay with blood."

"If that's the way you want it." The brown-haired man fired his weapon, and the gunman grabbed his left ear as it spurted blood. "From now on, people will call you 'earhole' — or something like that."

The gunman howled in pain but turned back to his adversary. "Put your gun away, and I'll kill you!"

"Than why should I do that?"

The gunman moved his right hand flashed for his pistol. "Do it!"

The other man fired a second shot. This one tore off the gunman's right thumb and smashed the hammer of the pistol under it.

The young gunman dropped to the floor, clutching the hole where his missing thumb had been. His ear continued to flush blood, too.

The man with the gun walked over and stood over the young gunman. "Is there a doctor in here?" he asked.

The bartender said, "Doc Pollman's office is down the street."

"Somebody go get him," the brown-haired man said.

A heavyset man rushed out of the saloon, and his footsteps were heard on the boardwalk.

"You shot me!" the gunman cried. "Twice!"

"You should thank me, young fella. I saved your life. You wanted blood — I gave you blood. You were about to murder that cowboy who apologized to you. You were looking for someone to kill."

"You blew off my thumb!"

"I gave you a chance to find out what you're best at. Gunfightin' sure ain't it. You'll live, so will the cowboy. And you get to start all over again. You'll always have that ear hole as a reminder. Grow up. Become a better man. You don't have to be a burr under everybody's saddle."

"What's your name?" the wounded man gasped.

"Stony Diamond."

Voices from around the saloon said, "The shootist?" "Stony Diamond?" "That young man is lucky to be alive."

CHAPTER 2

Stony Diamond had ridden Southeast from San Angelo to Junction on the Llano River. After all the shooting and killing in San Angelo, he had turned in his town marshal's badge and left. While it was never his plan, the stories of how he had cleaned up the town added to his reputation. Now at age 26, he was already known as "the Texas Shootist." The former seminary graduate and one-time pastor had become a gunfighter. It wasn't a title he ever wanted. Still, it was his.

The shooting of the loudmouth want-to-be gunfighter in Junction had been necessary, he thought. He couldn't allow a kid who had bumped into the man with the chip on his shoulder to be gunned down. Neither did he want to face the gunman in a fight that didn't need to happen. He'd done as little damage as he could to the hot head and left him alive.

Leaving Junction, Stony headed Southwest to Del Rio on the Rio Bravo, as it was known in Mexico, or the Rio Grande as Americans called it. Originally called San Felipe Springs, the town's name was changed to San Felipe Del Rio because local lore said the name came from early Spanish explorers who offered a mass at the site on St. Philip's Day, 1635. St. Philip was one of the Twelve Apostles.

In 1883, local residents called for a post office. The United States Postal Department shortened "San Felipe del Rio" to "Del Rio" to avoid confusion with San Felipe de Austin.

It was a Texas town not a built around a square like those in Mexico. It had 3 streets, 4 if you counted the one cross street. Businesses were lined up on both sides of the primary street which was wide enough to allow a wagon or stage to turn around.

Del Rio was a town divided against itself — a town of two feuding families. But Stony's reason for being in Del Rio was to find a gambler and saloon owner named Sloan Rush. It was the only lead he had to locate a sister he barely remembered.

Stony had been left in a Ft. Worth orphanage as a

toddler by his young teenage sister, whom he only vaguely remembered. About all he knew was that she saved his life because as little more than a child herself, she could never have cared for him. According to the records, her name was Crystal Agate Diamond. He didn't know who their father or mother had been but hoped to get some answers from his sister.

The dry, dusty town was half adobe, half wooden with a few tent businesses scattered. Work had started on a church at the North end of the main street but it was only a frame at the moment. Stony left his dark chestnut with a flaxen main and tail at a livery and took his Winchester and his saddlebags with him. Katty-corner from the Catholic church, across both the main street but also the cross street was Hollett House Hotel. He mounted the boardwalk in front of the two-story abode building and entered.

"Buenos dias," the young Mexican behind the check-in desk said. Stony nodded and said, "Morning."

The young man, dressed in a white shirt and string tie with garters on his forearms, looked Stony over and switched to English. "Whittenburg or Crenshaw?" he asked.

"Beg pardon?" Stony asked.

"Which side are you with?"

"Side?"

"Marsh Whittenburg or Theo Crenshaw."

Gunfire was heard from outside. Two pistol shots followed by a third.

The desk clerk ducked down behind his desk as Stony crossed quickly to the open front doors. Stony pulled his .44 revolver and carried his Winchester with him as he stepped up beside one door and pushed it back against the adobe wall.

Out in the street, one man was down on a knee, taking careful aim with his pistol as blood leaked from a wound in his thigh. He was in his late teens — a cowhand. In the alley beside a wooden false front store, the other shooter had taken shelter but was holding his pistol up to a blood drooling left shoulder. This man, maybe 30, dressed in chaps and the well-worn range clothes, was hurrying down the alley away from the fight.

After a minute, two other armed men rushed to the aid of the shooter in the street. Stony holstered his pistol and stepped out on the boardwalk. The wounded man was helped to his feet and out of the road to a pharmacy. The sign read Pharmacy - La Farmacia and below that, Doctor - El Consultorio Mèdco.

"Sully Crenshaw," the desk clerk said from just inside the hotel. He was indicating the injured rider taken off the street. "They've taken him to Doc Negrete."

"Part of the feud?" Stony asked.

"That's why I asked which side you were on," the young clerk said.

"Neither."

"Pardòn, señor."

The clerk returned to his post, and Stony followed."

"This kind of thing happen often? I mean out in the street?"

"They try to kill each other where they can."

Stony shook his head in disbelief.

"How long will you be with us, señor?"

"I'm not sure. I'm looking for a man named Sloan Rush. Do you know him?"

"Sì. He owns The Silver Dollar."

"Saloon?"

"Sì. This side of the street." The clerk pointed left.

Stony signed the register, and the clerk handed him a key.

The clerk said, "Up the stairs and on the left."

"Bath?"

"I'll ready one for you, señor. It's at the end of the main hall."

"Much obliged."

Stony took the key and carried his rifle and saddlebags up to his room.

He laid out a suit, a clean shirt, and a tie on the bed. Then the clerk tapped on the door, saying, "Whenever you are ready, señor."

In the bath, Stony took his time to wash away the dirt and dust in the trail. He dressed in his black suit, gray shirt, and string tie. He put on his gun-belt and slipped his second revolver in the holster in the center of his back. Next, he put on his black vest and frock coat. When he was ready, Stony rolled up this trail clothes and left them on the floor outside his room door. He mentioned it to the clerk before he left for The Silver Dollar.

CHAPTER 3

The Silver Dollar saloon was cool inside. The adobe double story building had 2 feet thick outside walls. These insulated the bar from the border heat and even the few cold spells from time to time. The bar's woodwork and that behind it were as intricate as the staircase and the tables around the room. Two multi-lamp chandeliers lit the room, which had only two windows.

Stony crossed to the room to the zinc topped bar. He saw a gambler playing solitaire across the room in the promenade and ornately carved mirror behind the bar.

"Whisky?" the Mexican bartender asked with only a slight Spanish accent.

"Beer," Stony said.

Two soiled Doves sat at a back table by themselves. A younger girl, maybe 12 or 13, with freckles and tied back wavy coffee brown hair was cleaning the tables and chairs.

Nodding at the image in the glass, Stony asked. "Sloan Rush?"

The bartender nodded and set a cold foamy beer on the bar. Stony took a sip, tossed a nickel on the bar, and walked across to the owner.

Sloan Rush wore a broadcloth vest over his white shirt and silk puff tie. His sleeves were folded almost up to his elbows. He had an ivory-handled pistol in a shoulder holster.

"Mr. Rush," Stony said, stopping at the table.

Without looking up from his cards, the man said, "Mr. Diamond."

"I'd like to ask you a few questions if you don't mind."

"I do mind. These are working hours for me. If you want to sit down and play a hand or two, perhaps we can talk."

Stony pulled out a chair and sat. He pulled out his wallet as Rush looked over to the bartender saying, "Diego!"

The bartender brought over a box of stamp sealed card decks.

"Pick a deck," Rush said to Stony.

Stony picked a deck in the middle of the box. The bartender returned to his location as Rush nodded to Stony to open the deck. Stony broke the stamp and extracted the cards placing the deck face down on the table. Rush reached for the cards, flipped over the stack, and spread the cardboards across the table. He removed the two jokers, put them back in the box, and dropped the box into an empty wire wastebasket beside his chair. The gambler restacked the cards and began shuffling them. After a half dozen shuffles, Rush stopped, triple cut the deck, and said, "Deal."

Stony restacked the three piles, reshuffled the cards. Next, he burned the top card by flipping the 9 of spades off the top, showing it to Rush, and placed it face-up on the bottom of the deck.

Stony dealt a hand of five card stud to Rush and himself.

Sloan Rush was 58, lean, receding salt and pepper hair, a strong nose, and dark hooded eyes. He wore no rings on his long fingers.

Both men tossed a dollar in the center of the table as their ante. When all cards were dealt, the first to both face down and the last 4 face up, the men looked at their hold card. Rush opened for three dollars, Stony saw the bit and raised 2 dollars.

The gambler saw Stony's raise and bumped him with a $10 bet. The game continued until the pot was up to almost $50, and Rush called.

Both men flipped over their hold card and Stony won with a full house, 3 8s over a pair of 4s.

The deal passed to Sloan Rush. After three shuffles Rush pushed the deck to Stony to cut it. Stony just tapped the deck with his index finger meaning he accepted the shuffle as it was.

Rush dealt with the deck on the table after he had burned the first card. He used his thumb to slide each card off the top of the deck, gripped it with index finger and thumb.

Stony won the second hand with a pot of near $80. Rush claimed the next two pots.

After a half-hour of play, when it was Stony's deal again, Rush asked, "So you have questions?"

"I do," Stony said, dealing cards. "I'm looking for my sister — Crystal Diamond."

Rush paused before he picked up his hold card. He thought for a moment and anted up. Then he asked, "Middle name?"

"Agate. Crystal Agate Diamond."

Stony covered the ante with his own dollar, and Rush dealt.

"She hasn't used that name in years," Rush said.

"What name does she use?"

"Bouvier. Crystal Bouvier." Then, without a pause, he said, "Dealer raises $20."

"I'll see your 20 and bump you another 20."

"That's $20 to me," Rush said, "and I'll see you and raise another 10."

Stony didn't react to the card play. He saw the raise and called.

Rush won the hand.

"How well do you know her?" Stony asked.

"Well, enough to know she doesn't have a brother."

"So, not that well."

"You might be surprised," Rush said as he pulled the money from the pot into his pile of cash. He handed the cards to Stony.

"She left me at an orphanage in Ft. Worth when I was just starting to walk."

"You don't say?"

"Do you know where she is?"

"Yes. But that doesn't mean I'm telling you."

"Why not?"

"Mister, I don't know you. I know the name you use and the reputation that goes along with it. But I'm not about to break Crystal's confidence."

"Maybe I'll just hang around and talk to her myself."

"Be ready for a long wait. She's not in Del Rio."

The batwing doors slammed open, and one of

the two cowboys who had helped the wounded man out of the street looked around. "Stony Diamond?" he called.

The man, 40s with a long and shaggy mustache, got a nod toward the only busy table in the saloon from the bartender. He strode across the room as Stony got to his feet.

"You Stony Diamond? The shootist?"

"Speak your piece," Stony said.

"I'm askin' if you're working for Marsh Whittenburg?"

"I'm not working for anybody."

"Will you ride out and talk to Mr. Crenshaw? I'm sure he'd make it worth your while."

"I'm not getting involved in this feud if that's what you're asking?"

The man clenched his jaw and said, "The fact is — if you're not on our side, you again' us." The cowhand whirled on his heels and stalked out.

"I'll say this for you," Sloan Rush said, "you do know how to make friends."

Stony finished his beer, collected his money and left the Silver Dollar.

Rush took the cards and began play Solitaire as the young girl walked up to him.

"Was that Stony Diamond?"

"That's what he said."

"Anything else?"

"Yeah. He claimed to be your uncle."

The girl looked up and then back at Rush.

"Mother never said anything about having a brother."

"No she didn't."

CHAPTER 4

Outside The Silver Dollar, Stony stood on the boardwalk and thought for a moment. He scanned the buildings up and down the street. His eyes settled on a storefront with a sign reading, "The Del Rio Post" past the cross street. He crossed the road, and walked down to the newspaper office. He opened the door and stepped inside.

A middle-aged woman, 40, slightly overweight, a pencil stuck in the dark blonde hair piled on top of her head, was looking in the drawer of a card catalog when the bell over the door clanged. She left the drawer open and crossed past a littered pair of desks to a railing separating the front of the operation from the working area.

"Afternoon," she said. "You must be Stony Diamond."

Stony nodded his agreement.

"We hear you didn't come to town to join in our current unpleasantness."

"Is that what you're calling it?"

"In this business, we have to use whatever metaphors we can to keep from getting caught in the crossfire." She offered her hand to Stony. "Alvira Maxon," she said.

Stony removed his hat and shook her right hand, noting the ring on her left hand. "Mrs. Maxon."

"Please. It's Alvira. What can we do for you?"

"Information."

"That's our business. Shoot."

"Is there a Crystal Agate Diamond or Crystal Bouvier in Del Rio?"

The lady scrunched her mouth and closed her eyes in thought. She tilted her head and then slowly shook it as she spoke. "Neither are names I've ever heard." She turned to the obese Mexican typesetter filing used lead type into drawers. "Jaime," she called. "You ever know of a Crystal Diamond or a Crystal Bouvier?"

"No, señora," the man said after a moment through full chapped lips.

"Kin of yours?" Alvira asked Stony.

"Sister — but she might not even know I'm alive. She left me in an orphanage when I was very young."

"I'll ask Tate when he gets back from making deliveries. He's my husband. He's got a better memory than me -- I'm sorry t' say."

"I appreciate your help."

"Want us to run a story in next week's edition? Maybe somebody else in these parts knows."

"I'd rather you didn't. This is private business."

"I understand. But if you change your mind — let us know."

"Thank you."

"Someone you might check with is Father Ochoa down at the Catholic Church. He grew up in Acuña — the town across the Rio from us — well, on a ranch over there actually."

"Father Ochoa. Good idea." Stony tipped his hat and walked outside.

***

Our Lady of Sorrows Catholic Church was the first religious structure built in Del Rio. While most of the Hispanic residents were Catholic, the majority of the anglos were protestant — but so far, no church had been completed. Still, some of the anglos were Catholic having families which had come from Ireland and Scotland.

The adobe whitewashed Catholic Church had a faded red-orange tiled roof. Inside, it, like The Silver Dollar, was pleasant. The dozen dark wooden pews and alcoves were lit by burning candles. Images of the Holy Family and saints were painted on the walls. Above the altar hung a 6-foot hand-carved cross with a crude image of the crucified Jesus on it.

Stony came in with his hat in his hand and took a seat on the last row of pews. He noticed two older women dressed in all black were praying in different alcoves. A young woman came out of the confessional, genuflected, and walked out into the sunlight. A minute or so later, a mostly bald man in his late 60s stepped out of the other side of the confessional. A ribbon stoll hung around his neck and down his white cotton robe. He had craggy features with deep hazel eyes in an oval-shaped face. His leather sandals were quiet as he made his way up the side aisle and moved around behind Stony. He sat in the pew in front of Stony and turned back to face him.

"You must be the gunfighter everyone is talking about," the priest said in only slightly accented English.

"I didn't mean to cause a disturbance," Stony said.

"No disturbance. New faces in town are just grist for the gossip mill. I hear you'd declared yourself neutral in the feud."

"It's none of my affair, Father. And I didn't come here to become involved."

"That is good to know."

"You are Father Ochoa, correct?"

"I am. And if the stories are true, you used to be a minister."

"Yes."

"How does one go from being a servant of God to a gunfighter?"

"God has many servants, Father. Wasn't David a servant of God when he killed Goliath – Gideon when he fought the Midianites?"

"Yes, but God told us, "Vengeance is mine. I will repay."

"When a member of my church got drunk and murdered his wife and children — and the local law said it was out of his jurisdiction — I knew it was not out of God's jurisdiction."

The priest was silent until he finally said, "It is not for me to judge. I've not walked in your shoes, so I will not try to now."

Stony nodded his head but said nothing.

"Is there something I can do for you, my son?"

"I am looking for my sister. I don't know what happened to my parents — or even who they were. When I was very young, my sister took me to an orphanage — and left me there."

"And you are angry about that?"

"Not at all. She was little more than a child herself. She saved my life. I want to find her and thank her — perhaps do something for her I couldn't do as a child."

The priest considered Stony's words and placed a weathered hand on the gunfighter's arm.

"How can I help?"

"The lady at the newspaper says you have been here longer than her or her husband. Have you ever heard the name Crystal Diamond — or perhaps Crystal Bouvier?"

There was a troubled expression that descended on the priest's face. He removed his arm and slowly said, "I'm sorry, my son. I've heard the name — but I am bound by the confessional not to reveal anything else I know."

"Can you tell me if she lives somewhere around here?"

"No. I'm sorry. There's nothing more I can tell you."

CHAPTER 5

Stony's next stop was the physician who had treated the leg wounded cowboy who was shot out in the road. He walked up the dusty street and onto the boardwalk when 6 riders thundered into town. They pulled up in front of the doctor's office and pharmacy. They all dismounted except their leader. That broad-shouldered man had a jowly face and deep-set eyes. He wore a wide striped broadcloth vest and a cross-draw pistol on his left hip.

"Stony Diamond?" the man asked in a ragged voice.

"I am," Stony said as the ranch hands gathered 2 on his left and three on his right.

"Elsworth Whittenburg," the rancher said, still in the saddle.

"And?" Stony asked, unimpressed.

"Is it true you ain't workin' for Theo Crenshaw?"

"I don't know him any more than I know you."

"Well, before you ask, I'm not hiring gun-fighters."

"I didn't ask."

"I can make sure he stays out it, Pa?" A cocky younger version of the rancher said. He was just out of his teens from the look of him, had a low slung pistol, and was a lady's man it appeared from his swagger.

"Don't go buyin' trouble, Wylie. We've a plate full as it is. The man says he's not in this — I'll take him at his word."

"I won't," the kid said, going for his gun.

But Stony's .44 S & W American was out, cocked and aimed at Wylie's chest before the younger man could get his shiny Colt out of his holster. The boy froze. Stony didn't move as the realization sank into Wylie's mind that he could be dead, or at best, gasping his last breath.

All the men waited in anticipation. It was clear Wylie had pulled first, and Stony had every right to kill the kid whose blood drained from his face.

"Let go of the pistol, Wylie," Elsworth Whittenburg said, "— slowly. And put the thong back on the hammer. If the man wanted to kill you, he would have by now."

Wylie did as instructed, trying to swallow but finding his mouth and throat too parched to respond. When he was done, he raised his hands shoulder high.

Stony lowered his pistol to his waist as he turned back to Whittenburg and eyed the rest of the riders.

"Mount up," Whittenburg told his men. The men followed their leader's command, slowly and carefully. When the men were all back in the saddle, Marsh tipped his hat to Stony. The group pulled away and rode up the road to The Silver Dollar.

❧

As the group of riders turned, Stony holstered his revolver.

"Señor Diamond," a voice said from inside the *farmacia*.

Stony turned to find a short Mexican with a thin mustache. His hair was dark and cut short, the man had a receding chin and a broad nose.

"Doctor?" Stony asked.

"People call me that, but I am no trained doctor. I am a *herbalista*."

Stony saw open bins of plants and bottles on the shelf of leaves and roots.

"I heal with the plants God has given us," he continued in reasonably good English but still a pronounced Spanish accent. "I can set most broken bones, help when there's no midwife available. But there are many things I cannot heal or even help."

"I saw they brought the man shot in the street to you," Stony said.

"I can often stop bleeding — dig out bullets — or know when to leave them where they are."

"Smarter than some doctors I've met."

"Enrique Negrete," the man stuck out his hand. Stony shook it. "How can I help you, señor?"

"I'm looking for someone. A woman. Crystal Diamond. Maybe Crystal Bouvier."

The man thought for a moment but moved his head from left to right as he said, "Pardòn, señor, but I have never heard of this woman."

"And you treat people from all around here?"

"*Sí*. They call me Doc Negrete. And I go to all the ranches and farms. Even across the Rio."

Stony sighed as he digested the disappointment.

"I mean no disrespect, señor, but have you to spoken to Miss Kensler?"

"Kensler?" Stony asked.

"Miss Leola Kensler. She is — how you say — the owner of — *casa del puta*. Cathouse."

"Ah. No, I haven't. I was going to see you, and the local sheriff, first."

"Señor Glasford is not in town. Could be back tomorrow."

Stony looked outside and saw the day's shadows were getting long.

"Thank you for your time, señor Negrete. Can you suggest a good place to eat?"

"The Cantina near the river. *Excelente comida.* Very good food."

"I'll give it a try."

"He will most likely tell you the same thing I have, but you could ask señor Alonso Huerta if he knows."

"Thank you again — Doc."

As he was leaving, Stony was hailed by a stocky man who wore a bowler hat and had a neatly trimmed beard and mustache.

"Tate Maxon," he identified himself. "My wife asked me to find you and see if I could help."

"Thank you, sir," Stony said as the two men shook hands.

"I'm sorry to say I don't know anything that

can help you. Alvira filled me in and asked me to make sure I found you and at least let you know I don't know any more than she remembers."

"I'm obliged for your time, Mr. Maxon."

"Good luck in your search. My experience is that if you keep turning over rocks, sooner or later you'll find what you're looking for."

"That's my hope," Stony said.

CHAPTER 6

For the first time that day, Stony was glad he wore a frock coat. As the sunset, Del Rio cooled as it steadily gave up its accumulated heat of the day. He took a table on the patio enclosed on three sides by a low adobe wall at The Cantina. A lovely Mexican girl in a white off the shoulders, colorful cotton dress stepped up to his table.

"*Buena Noches, señor.*" She then switched to English — perfect English. "What can I get for you?"

"Coffee, and something good to eat."

"Everything my papá makes is good, señor." The dimples in both cheeks deepened as she smiled, and her dark eyes seem to flash.

"Then what would you suggest?"

"Beef enchiladas, charro beans, rice — and Tequila."

She was both lissome and petite.

"I'd prefer coffee," Stony said.

"*Si, señor.*" Something held them looking at each other.

Stony asked, "When your father has a moment, would you ask him if he'd come to speak with me?"

"Right away, señor." She left in a swirl of her skirt with a coltish feminine walk.

She returned with his meal and coffee several minutes later. She served it with a radiant smile. She had a cup looped in one finger as she clutched a steaming pot by a pad covered handle.

"Papá will join you as soon as he can."

"*Gracias, señorita,*" Stony said.

There was a delight in her eyes at his Spanish, and her dimples deepened.

The food was as delicious as both the local doctor and Stony's waitress had predicted.

Halfway through his meal, a sinewy Mexican man in his late 40s approached Stony's table.

"*Señor, Diamond,*" he spoke in a deep but hoarse voice as he pulled out a chair and sat.

"*Gracias, señor Huerta,*" Stony said, wiping his mouth with his cloth napkin.

"My daughter, Teresa, told me you wish to talk to me?" The man had a scar across the bottom of his throat. Stony suspected someone had tried to cut the man's throat sometime in the distant past.

"Yes," Stony said, making sure he remembered the girl's name, Teresa. He explained about his search for his sister.

Alonso Huerta listened intently but, at the end, shook his head.

"Sorry, señor, but those are names I have never heard.

Stony nodded in resignation. "Gracias, I appreciate your talking to me."

"I only wish I could have been of some help."

"Thank you anyway. And as your daughter and Doc Negrete both said, your food is excellent."

"Gracias," Huerta said as he stood and walked away.

Stony enjoyed the rest of his meal and two additional cups of coffee. He would have blushed if he had to admit he also enjoyed watching Teresa Huerta flit about the patio serving him and the other customers.

As he paid for his meal and left, he saw inside The Cantina the gambler, and saloon owner, Sloan Rush, was eating inside with young girl who had been cleaning the tables at The Silver Dollar. He also picked up on the fact that the girl's eyes followed him.

☙❧

The local whore house was simply called "Red House." It was a two-story wooden building with only a couple of horses at the hitching rail. Stony took the doorknob in his hand, as seen in the light of the red lantern hanging from a porch post, and opened it.

No one was there to greet him, but the air was filled with the sound of a tiny piano with more than one key clearly out of tune. He removed his hat as he stepped across the worn rug and looked into the parlor where a bony black man wearing a bowler hat, white shirt with garters high up on his sleeves pounding out "Buffalo Gals" on the keys.

Three soiled doves lounged with their legs spread across stuffed chairs. They wore half laced corsets and flimsy nightgowns. Both were smoking thin cigars.

"Welcome to Red House," a husky female voice said behind him.

Stony turned to find a stout red-headed woman of 30 or so, with ample endowments on full display. "What's your pleasure?" she asked, jiggling her breasts. "Full house or just a handful?"

"I'd rather talk."

The woman let her breasts drop back into her corset. "Talkin' or pokin' — a half-hour still cost $2."

"Are you Leola Kensler?"

"I am."

"You're the one I want to talk to."

"Let's go cowboy," she said, taking Stony's arm and turning toward the stairs.

"A table and chairs are all we need," he said, holding back.

"Well," she said, looking at him curiously, "there's the dining room."

"That will do," he said.

She redirected him down the hall past the stairs and the parlor to a room with a 12 person table and chairs. She let him sit at the head of the table and sat back, pulling her skirt up, exposing her naked thighs above her striped stockings.

Stony repeated to her the same story he'd given Sloan Rush, Alvira Maxon at the newspaper office, Father Ochoa, Doc Negrete, Tate Maxon in the street, and Alonso Huerta at the cantina.

"I'm afraid I've got a short straw for you, too," Leola Kensler said after giving up on her hope of drawing Stony upstairs. "There's a lot of pillow talk here, and I make sure the girls let me in on all of it.

But I've got nothing I can tell you. Never heard either name."

Stony sighed and got to his feet fishing $2 from his vest and stacking them on the table. But Leola pushes the silverback towards Stony.

"I hardly give you your money's worth," she said. "I may be a whore, but I'm an honest one."

"I consider your time worth the expense," Stony said. "For all I know, my sister was a soiled dove herself. I don't know how else she could have made her way in the world after leaving me. You keep the money — for her sake."

Leola scooped up the coins and deposited them between her breasts as she got to her feet.

She walked Stony back to the front door. He stepped outside and put on his hat. But as he started to walk away, she called out, "Hold on a second. Maybe this ain't worth anything, but — I didn't always run this place. Philomena Dinwiddie — now Philomena Shaddon owned it before me. I worked for her til' she married Witt Shaddon. She sold the place t' me."

"Do you know where I can find — Mrs. Shaddon?"

"Sure. The Shaddon ranch is in Carrizo Springs — about a hundred miles southeast as the crow flies."

"Witt and Philomena Shaddon. Thank you, Miss Leola."

"It could be a dead-end, too."

"It's another stone I need to overturn. But at least I'll have a look-see. Thank you. I consider my money well spent."

CHAPTER 7

The gullies, ravines, and coulees of the Texas landscape had been places of shelter and escape for cattle for over a century. The Spanish had brought the forbearers of the breed to the arid Southwest. Texas's rugged and hostile lands had forced the lost or miss placed animals to develop into independent and defiant longhorns. Instead of docile and domestic cattle, those that wandered away, or somehow escaped their herders, adapted. Just as newcomers struggled with the native savages, the loose cattle learned to deal with the threats of natural predators, droughts, flash floods, or the blue norther that occasionally turned the land into a freezing death trap. The hardy survivors took to the slashes in the land for shade in the summers and shelter in the blasts of winter.

The law of the range was that any unbranded bull, cow, or calf belonged to he who could capture it. But even branded cattle would meander back to the cuts in the land and the stalwart, twisted bushes and trees such places produced. It was the cowboy's job to find and root out such renegades or any unclaimed cattle they could find.

Dogleg Canyon Northeast of Del Rio wasn't so much a canyon as it was an enlarged gulch with many switch backs and crevices in the open range. When bush poppers, the cowboys assigned to the recovery and discovery task from both sides of the local feud, encountered each other, a gunfight broke out. Revolvers and Winchesters were emptied and reloaded for half an hour.

In the end, a half-dozen men on each side recovered their dead and wounded and fell back.

"Who got hit?" Rufus Crenshaw, the head of the clan's second youngest son, called when the smoke had dissipated.

"I caught one in the foot," Lucian, the very youngest of the Crenshaw boys, said. "Gil was knocked off his horse, but I think he'll live. It's Ernest they killed."

"Ernest," the chiseled faced Rufus said. Ernest was a cousin by marriage but still a member of the family.

"I'll bet it was the gunfighter that got him," the kid said, checking his boot."

"Thought he said he was stayin' out of this."

"Who else on the Whittenburg side can shoot like that?"

"I'll get my Sharps and put an end to that son of a bitch," Silent March said. The man had hardly spoken 10 words since the war. He was known for his brooding silence. Either he had done something in the war or had seen something which profoundly affected him. Nobody knew which. He kept to himself and did more than his share of the work.

"How you doin', Lucian?" Rufus asked.

"My boots are filling up with blood, but I can ride."

"Let get back to the ranch." the young leader said.

The hulking March slid to the ground and boosted Lucian on to the hurricane deck of his horse.

"March," Rufus said, "we'll leave this up to you."

The day of the Dogleg Canyon fight, Stony was on the trail Southeast. He wore a duster to cover his dark coat and pants and rode hard all day. He made camp that night near a seeping spring. Before dawn the next day, he was riding again.

From directions he got from a traveling tinker, Stony was able to find the Shaddon ranch. As he rode into the ranch yard, he saw that the place was well taken care of and in order. All the buildings painted, all the gear stored in predesignated places in the open barn.

He pulled to a halt and waited. "Hello, the house," Stony called out just as he entered the gate. Two ranch hands came out of the barn with implements in their hands from their current jobs.

An older man, over 60 but athletic and displaying only a slight paunch, stepped out on the main house's porch. His hair was all white and thinning from the crown forward.

"Afternoon, stranger," the man, Witt Shaddon, Stony figured, said in a friendly drawl. "What's your business?"

"Witt Shaddon?" Stony asked.

"That's me," the square-jawed, clean-shaven man said.

"If you'll permit me, I'd like to speak to your wife."

"Philomena? She know you?"

"No, sir, I've not had the pleasure. I've ridden down from Del Rio with a couple of questions for her about my sister."

"And your name?"

"Stony Diamond."

"The gunfighter?"

"Yes, sir."

The man thought about it for a moment before he called, "Have you had anything to eat?"

"Not since last night on the trail."

"Then come on in. Isom," he called to the barn, "come take care of the man's horse."

The black cowboy parked his rake against the barn door and stepped out as Stony rode in.

"It must be pretty important for you to come this far," the rancher said as Stony stepped down and shed his duster.

"It is, sir — to me."

"Well, come on in and let's see if we can't do something for you."

"May I leave my duster on the chair out here?" Stony asked as he climbed the steps.

"I'm sure the wife will appreciate it."

"I think I'm still pretty dusty," Stony said, looking down at his pants and brushing some of the dust away."

"No more than what she's used to, young fellow — but she does like a tidy house." The rancher held open the front door and called inside, "Philomena, we've got a hungry visitor!"

CHAPTER 8

Philomena Shaddon was 45, full-figured, high cheekbones, dove gray hair which matched her eyes. She turned to Stony and indicated that he should sit as she said, "Welcome," in a husky voice. "No man leaves my table without a full belly. Care for some buttermilk?"

"Yes, please," Stony said, taking a chair at the kitchen table.

"You've come a long way, young man," Witt said, pulling a pipe out of his vest pocket. This must be important."

"It is to me, Mr. Shaddon."

"Call me Witt," the rancher said.

"And I'm Philomena," his wife said over her shoulder at the stove.

"I hope I'm not going to be an embarrassment with my questions?"

"Don't worry on it, son. We value honesty around here above anything else. And I got a good read on you when you said you were a gunfighter without any hesitation. It shows character."

"Thank you," Stony said.

"Here you go," Philomena said, as she set a plate of ham, cornbread, and beans in front of Stony. "Take a few bites to let your stomach know your throat ain't been cut," she winked at him and took a seat.

Stony did eat a little and relished the buttermilk.

"Now what can I do for you," "Philomena asked as Witt took a chair near her.

Stony told his story and included the fact that he had been directed to Philomena by Leola Kensler."

"Leola Kensler," Philomena clapped her hands in delight. "How's she doing, and how's Red House holding up? That's were Witt and I met, you know."

"No, I didn't," Stony said. "But both Miss Kensler and Red House seem to be doing very well."

"Glad to hear it," Philomena said, reaching out for Witt's hand. "Now, what's that name again?"

"Crystal Agate Diamond," Stony said slowly. "Or maybe Crystal Bouvier."

Philomena thought for a moment wrinkling her forehead as she did.

"I think so," she finally said. "It's been a long time — but — if I remember right, it was Sloan Rush who said it. It was right after he first came t' town. Before he bought The Silver Dollar."

This got Stony's interest to the point he put down his fork to listen.

"He came in one night — raging drunk — and mad as hell. He kept shouting, 'Crystal Agate, why did you do it?' He never did get around to saying what 'it' was. But he was mad at her for something. It took two of the girls and two days before he was himself again. He was a regular customer for one of the girls, Florrie, I think. Yes, it was Florrie. Florrie Stults."

"Do you know where she is now?"

"Oh, hon, she's dead. Fell off a horse and broke her neck the next year, I think it was."

"Did she ever say anything about Crystal?"

"Not that I recall. If I were to guess, I'd say Crystal did Sloan wrong somehow — and he must have loved her to have taken it so hard. But that's just my idea."

"I'd take it as gospel," Witt said. "Philomena knows men."

"That's how I knew Witt needed more than just an occasional roll in the hay," she said, patting his hand.

"And she knew she was the right one for me," Witt said with a smile.

"Go on and finish eating," Philomena said to Stony.

He finished his meal, and she gave him a slice of fresh apple pie.

When he had finished, Stony stood up.

"I appreciate both of you for your time. I think I need to get back to Del Rio and have another talk with Sloan Rush."

"There's no hurry," Witt said. "Stay the night and start fresh in the morning. Your horse would appreciate it."

"Well, thank you," Stony said. "Is there a spare bed in the bunkhouse?"

"We have a guest room," Philomena said. "It ain't used a lot, but it's yours for the night if you like."

"I'd have to be a fool to turn that offer down."

Stony sat on the front porch and helped Philomena shell peas while Witt tended to the ranch for the rest of the afternoon. He had a good supper and enjoyed the evening with the pair. That night he didn't get to sleep soon enough to miss the squeaking bedsprings coming from across the hall. Neither could he miss the sounds of delight from both Witt and his wife.

He had breakfast with the smiling couple and rode out as the sun was coming up.

Elm Creek near Eagle Pass was where Stony camped for the night. The next morning he rode through the ravines and coulees toward Del Rio. After climbing out of one of the dry arroyos, Stony felt he was being watched. He scanned the boulders and outcroppings when his saddle jerked, and his horse frog hopped. He saw a fresh gash in the leather below his saddle horn on the seat swell. He was able to grab the butt of his Winchester as he heard the rifle report. He tumbled out of the saddle, hit the ground, and rolled behind a boulder.

He peeked over the boulder with a fresh round levered into his rifle and saw the rifle flash a good 600 yards away. He pulled back before the fired round ricocheted off the rock near his head. He took off his black hat and began to make his way through the shadows and the rocks. His duster was the same color as the rocks, and by keeping to the shadows, he was able to make his way to a long gash in the ground that was deep enough to provide shade and cover. He was going to flank his would-be dry-gulcher.

CHAPTER 9

Silent Hogan March had spent the first years of the War of Northern Aggression with Bloody Bill Anderson. The Confederate volunteer guerrilla partisans targeted Union loyalists and federal soldiers in Missouri and Kansas. But there reached a point in which Hogan could no longer stomach the slaughter, rape, senseless pillaging of farmers. He deserted the group. In an attempt to redeem himself, he joined up as a regular Confederate soldier in Arkansas.

He was sent to Lee's Army of Northern Virginia, and because he had acquired a Yankee Sharps rifle, he was assigned to hunt wildlife to feed the troops. He was also told to dispatch targets of opportunity. He tried to stick to hunting but soon found himself seeking out Union troops whenever possible.

The event that most defined his life was when he spotted a Union officer 300 yards away squatting near a tree. It had become an unspoken rule among the ordinary soldiers on both sides of the conflict not to engage anyone in the process of dealing with the rampant Dysentery and chronic diarrhea.

Hogan March held his fire until the man stood up. Then March drilled the man in his lower back. As the Yankee twisted around, March saw the clerical collar the man wore with his uniform. March also discovered a child falling back with a bullet hole in her head. The Union chaplain had been feeding a starving child. March's bullet had pierced the man's body and also killed the girl as well.

From that moment on, Hogan March had become "Silent March." He didn't speak unless absolutely necessary. He did his job — hunting game — and never shot at another soldier from then to Lee's return from the Appomattox Courthouse.

He made his way back to Texas and found his uncle, Theophilus (Theo) Crenshaw. He took a job as a cowboy and quietly applied himself to that hard life. He was a top hand but not a leader. No job was too lowly nor too demanding. He was working for his redemption once more and thought he'd never fire a gun in anger again. The gunfight in Dogleg Canyon changed that with the death of his distant cousin Ernest.

For the past three days, he had taken up a position along the most likely route from Carrizo Springs and Del Rio. He waited through two sweltering days for the appearance of Stony Diamond. The gunfighter had gone to Carrizo Springs, March was told but returned in the next few days. March had almost given up when the Texas Shootist rode into view into the flat ground between boulders shoved up from below the ground sometime back and prehistory.

Sweat ran down March's face and into his eyes as he took a bead and a small lead on the rider. He was using the breech-loading .45 - 50 paper cartridge version. The rifle was still developing and a newer version but took the metal cartridge. Yet, the rifle had built its reputation on long distance accuracy. He wasn't sure if he hit the rider or if Stony had leaped off his jumping horse after March's shot.

A second shot Hogan March fired chipped a chunk of rock off the boulder behind which Stony had taken refuge. March kept looking for the gunman and firing occasional shots whenever he thought he saw a glimpse of movement in the rocks across the way.

Stony had learned the first rule of sniping in the war was "shoot and move." Muzzle flashes could reveal a shooter's location. Whoever was trying to kill Stony didn't know this truth. The man had stayed in the same place and had fired several rounds. Stony was able to pinpoint his advisory's hiding place.

As Stony crawled along the gash in the ground, he made a point of staying in the shadow of the ditch's lip. He also moved slowly so as not to leave a dust trail. It took him over an hour to cross the open ground and get up behind the shooter.

When Stony finally was able to lay his eyes on this would-be murder, he raised his Winchester and crept around until he had a clear shot.

"Leave the rifle there," Stony commanded, sighting down his iron sights. "Stand up slowly — and you'll live through this."

Hogan March lifted his left hand slowly. How had the man gotten behind him? As he got to his knees, he whipped around with the heavy slant-breech Sharps in his right hand. But he was dead before he could bring his weapon into play. Stony shot him in the center of his chest and promptly levered a second round into his Winchester's chamber and added that slug to the first in the killer's body. March's heart was ripped apart, and he sprawled back against the site he had used to brace his rifle.

Stony stepped forward and examined the man. He didn't know who he had killed — only that the man was clearly trying to kill him.

An unsaddled grulla grazed near a pond nearby. Stony collected the horse and the rider's tack from under a cottonwood tree. Stony saddled the horse, loaded the body across the saddle — which took a little doing. Horses don't like the smell of blood and that of their rider, especially. Finally, Stony got March draped over the saddle and secured. He collected the Sharps and his own Winchester and climbed up behind the saddle. The horse didn't seem overburdened as Stony pointed him back to the opening, where he could get his own horse. He mounted and led the dry gulches across his saddle to Del Rio.

Once in town, Stony took the dusty main street, the office of Sheriff Nils Glasford. Three local boys had seen Stony leading a horse with a dead man across another horse and had followed. A couple of other townfolk starred in shock at the sight.

The Sheriff, 60s, drooping mustache and a slash of beard from his lower lip down past this chin, stepped out of his office. He wore a dark checkered vest on his athletic torso with his brass star of office gleaming in the sun. He was of average height and wore a single pistol in a left-handed cross-draw position hear his right hip.

"Alf," he said to the oldest of the three boys, "you go get Mr.Ensley. Park, you and Junior," he said to the two younger boys, "find Doc Negrete."

The boys ran off as directed, and the Sheriff lifted the head of the dead man, saying, "Hogan March. They call him 'Silent' March" He looked at Stony, "You find him or kill him."

"He found me," Stony said. "Tried to bushwhack me. I did kill him."

"You'd be Stony Diamond," the Sheriff said. "Sheriff Nils Glasford. I hear you wanted to talk to me?"

CHAPTER 10

Stony and Sheriff Glasford unlashed Hogan March's body and laid it out in the dirt street beside his grulla. More citizens gathered around the body. Tate Maxon, the newspaper editor, pushed his way growing throng and eased his bowler hat back on his head as he stepped up beside the body. Maxon had a hand-sized paper tablet in his left hand and a pencil in his right.

"That's Silent March, isn't it?" the editor asked the Sheriff without looking the lawman's way.

"He's not breathing as well as he was last time I saw him," the Sheriff replied as he searched through the dead man's pockets to find nothing but the making for some smokes. The Sheriff did remove the gunbelt and hang it on deadman's saddle horn.

A portly man in a black suit and top hat and blood shot eyes wormed his way through the crowd to the body.

"Toot," the Sheriff greeted the man.

"Sheriff." He looked down at the body. "Hogan March," he said to himself. "This is going to be hell to pay."

Doc Negrete arrived and knelt beside the body. The short Mexican examined the two holes in March's chest. The physician crossed himself and stood.

"Two rifle shots, I think, Sheriff."

"Winchester," Stony said. "From about 10 feet away. He wouldn't drop his Sharps."

The Doctor stood and nodded to the man in the top hat. "There is nothing I can do for him, Señor Ensley."

"I'll get my wagon," the undertaker said to the Sheriff and pushed his way through the crowd.

"That's all, folks," Sheriff Glasford said. "You've all seen dead men before. Go on about your business."

"You can read all about it in Friday's Post," Tate Maxon announced as the crowd broke up.

After a few minutes, only Stony, the Sheriff, and

the newspaper editor were left standing near the body.

"Let step back in the shade," Sheriff Glasford said. The other two men followed the elderly lawman up on the boardwalk and into the building's early afternoon shade cast. "Toot Ensley will bring a couple of boys, and they'll pick up the body in a few minutes."

"Is it all right if I just listen?" Maxon asked.

"For the moment." The Sheriff turned to Stony and asked, "You said he tried to bushwhack you?"

"Or dry gulch me," Stony said, "whichever way you like."

"Where? I gather it wasn't long ago?"

"About an hour or so East of here," Stony began. "I don't know if the place has a name, but I came up out of a dry arroyo with boulders on each side."

"That's likely Briles Pass. I'll check it out."

"There will be track there, and a chunk of rock shot off one bolder I hid behind. There's also a shallow ditch — I'd guess it to a flash flood stream bed. High boulders on both sides. March, is that his name?" Stony asked.

"Silent March. Most folks around these parts have never heard him say a word. He some kin to the Crenshaws."

"Well, you'll find his paper shell casings high up on the South side."

"The Crenshaws will be out for you," the newspaper editor said to Stony.

"I'll be taking the horse back to the Crenshaws. It might be a good idea for you to go with me," Sheriff Glasford said. "Let them know the straight of it."

"Don't mind if I do. Oh, I do plan to keep that Sharps," Stony said as he stepped out into the sun and unlaced the Sharps scabbard from March's horse.

"He ain't goin' to object," Glasford said.

Up the street from Stony sat Sloan Rush leaning against a porch post while one of his bartenders told what he'd heard standing with the crowd.

"You got a gunsmith in town?" Stony said back on the boardwalk.

"Never heard of a job Dexter Ailes couldn't handle."

"His office is right down from the newspaper," Maxon added.

"Any idea why he was after me?" Stony asked.

"Both sides of this feud have been on the prod since that little shootout in Dogleg Canyon," the Sheriff said.

"When was that?"

JACK R. STANLEY

"The same day you left for Carrizo Springs. That afternoon it was," Maxon said.

"I don't know anything about it," Stony said.

"Not much to tell," Sheriff Glasford said as he saw the hearse wagon start down the street toward them. "Both sides were out maverick hunting and ran into each other. Couple of men wounded on both sides — one man killed on the Crenshaw side. Ernest, I believe," the Sheriff looked over at Maxon, who was making notes.

"Ernest," the editor confirmed without looking up from his notes.

"That will be Toot Ensley," the Sheriff said as the enclosed and unadorned black wagon pulled up in front of the Sheriff's office.

Two Mexicans stepped down from the wagon, one from beside the driver, Ensley, and the other from the rear. They folded the dead man's arms across his chest and moved him over to a tarp they had spread out beside the corpse. They moved the body to the tarp and then folded it over him. Lastly, they lifted the body by a board under the tarp and slipped it into the back of the glass-windowed wagon.

Without a word, the two Mexicans remounted the wagon, and Toot Ensley turned the vehicle around and headed back up the street.

"You want to get a drink or anything before we

60

head out to the Crenshaws'," Sheriff Glasford asked Stony.

"I'd like to water my horse. March's ride is likely a little dry, too."

"Troff's right across the street."

"Mind if I tag along," Tate Maxon asked.

"Might be a good idea," the Sheriff said. "Could keep the Crenshaws from doing something stupid."

"I'll meet you at the livery," Maxon said, hurrying off.

"Tell Virge to saddle my horse, too," Glasford called after the editor who waved a hand in acknowledgment.

After Stony had watered both horses, he walked with the Sheriff to the livery stable.

"Thank you, Virge," the Sheriff said to the long-bow-legged holster taking the reins of a red dun.

"Glad t' help," Sheriff.

Maxon mounted a dappled gray. The trio rode North out of town and turned East with March's body and horse trailing behind.

CHAPTER 11

The Crenshaw ranch was expansive but not ostentatious. When Stony rode into the ranch yard with Sheriff Glasford and Tate Maxon, the Sheriff was leading Silent March's horse. It was mid-afternoon, and three ranch hands were watching a fourth work at breaking a piebald mustang in the fenced corral. One of the standing men had his arm in a sling. From the looks of him, Stony thought this was the man who was wounded in the Del Rio street gunfight with Sully Crenshaw.

"Theo Crenshaw!" Sheriff Glasford called as the group rode into the ranch yard and up to the main house.

The man on board the mustang grabbed a tall

gate fence post and let the horse buck on by itself. The man climbed down and joined the three who had been watching as the group walked up beside Hogan March's horse. Glasford handed the reins to one of the three.

"This is Silent March's grulla," the ranch hand said.

The front door to the main house opened, and a man in his mid-60s with a full white beard and only a fringe of white hair around his head walked up to the edge of the porch.

"Theo," the Sheriff said, "March is dead. Toot Ensley has the body. He's waiting to hear from you."

"How?" was the only question from the slightly hunched, oblong faced clan leader.

"He tried to dry gulch me," Stony said.

"And who in the hell are you?" Crenshaw demanded.

"Stony Diamond."

That seemed to answer several of the man's unspoken questions.

"He's not involved with your feud with the Whittenburgs. He was on his way to Carrizo Springs when your boys had that scuffle in Dogleg Canyon."

"That's March's Sharps, the man with his arm in a sling said, walking up behind Theo Crenshaw.

"Not anymore," Stony said.

"How's that?" Theo asked.

"Let's just say your man March bet his life on it — and lost."

"That's not right," the wounded man said.

"Shut up," Theo commanded.

"We brought back his horse," the Sheriff said. "It has your brand on it." The Sheriff looked around and called out to the youngest cowboy standing near — 19 by the look of him. "Arley, you want to take him? Theo Crenshaw nodded and the boy took the animal's reins.

"What are you doing here, Maxon?" the clan leader asked.

"Covering the news. Be sure to read about it on Friday."

No one said anything for a minute, then Theo spoke once more.

"You've delivered your news and the horse. You have any other business here, Glasford?"

"Not unless there's somebody here who put March up to this?"

Nothing was said.

"All right then. Let's consider this matter finished," the Sheriff said.

"It's ain't finished," Theo said.

"Any more of this kind of cowardly thing, Theo, and I'm comin' back for you."

"Bring an army if you want to try it."

"How many men have to die over this?" the Sheriff asked. "I count four so far — five counting March. When is enough enough?"

"When the Whittenburgs have quit and left the country!"

"All this," the newspaper editor asked in amazement, "over a cow — not even a cow — a calf. Unbranded. By range law, it belongs to whoever captures it. That would be the Whittenburgs."

"That calf was ours. Its momma had died, and it wandered off."

"It found another momma," the Sheriff said. "Only it was a Whittenburg cow."

"Don't matter. The calf was ours."

"Not by law — and not by common sense."

"What if the Post bought you another cow — a full-grown steer if you like," Tate Maxon asked, "would that stop all this?"

"Not unless it came from the Wittenburgs — along with an apology."

"That'll never happen," the Sheriff said.

"Then this little war of ours will never end," Theo said, crossing his arms over his chest and forcing himself to stand up straight.

"There are none so blind..." Maxon said.

The three riders turned, but Theo Crenshaw

called after them, "Don't come back — any of you — without an invite!"

The trio rode out and got on the trail back to town.

Out of nowhere, the Sheriff turned to Stony.

"You any kin of Joe Diamond?"

Stony regarded the Sheriff a moment and said. "I don't know. I've never heard of him."

"Oh, he's likely dead by now. But 30 years ago — back in New Orleans — I saw him fight. Fastest hands I've ever seen — before or since."

"A gunfighter?"

"No, no. A prizefighter. He'd take on any comers. Whipped 'em all."

"I could be related, I guess. I don't know who my parents were — either of them."

"That's why he's looking for his sister," Maxon said.

"Oh, yeah. What was the question you wanted to ask me?"

Stony filled the Sheriff in on his story and asked about Crystal — under both possible names.

"Sorry, son, but I never came across any Crystal. With a name like that, I'm sure I'd remember."

The rest of the ride back to Del Rio was silent.

Back at the hotel, Stony left his duster with the clerk and ask for another bath.

"It's so hot," the clerk said, "how'd you feel about a cool dip?"

"Sounds good. Where?"

The young man gave Stony directions to a spring pool outside of town. Stony liked the idea and got some clean clothes from his room and walked out of the hotel.

He located the pool and was soon neck deep in clear spring water. Grabbing the bar of soap he'd brought, he was enjoying a nice bath when he glanced up to see supple and petite Teresa Huerta, the lovely Mexican daughter of Alonso standing with her hands on her hips watching him.

"You have found my place, Señor Diamond," she cooed. "May I join you?"

Without waiting for his answer, she pulled off her colorful cotton dress and removed the combs from her hair. The dimples in both cheeks deepened when she saw that Stony enjoyed the sight of her nakedness beside the pool. Her dark eyes flashed as she waded in and asked to borrow his soap.

Stony was mesmerized as he watched her, knowing he should look away but was unable to.

Finally, she swam up beside him and put her arms around his neck. He couldn't help but kiss her. After a few moments of delight, he pulled away and asked, "Teresa, how old are you?"

"Eighteen," she said with a seductive smile.

"I'm almost 10 years older than you."

"My mama is 15 years younger than my papa. She always told me to find a man who was not a silly boy. I think I have."

She pulled herself up to him, and they kissed again. They made love in the pool and again in the grass as the sun started to go down.

"I think you were hungry — for more than food," she laughed as they kissed once more.

CHAPTER 12

Teresa was dressed and gone before Stony had dried off and gotten into his clean clothes. He took his dirty clothes back to the hotel, left them with the clerk, and went straight to the cantina. He stood, hat in hand, waiting for Alonso Huerta outside the cantina's back door. When the owner and cook noticed Stony waiting for him, he wiped his hands on his apron and joined Stony outside.

"*Pardòn Señor Huerta*," Stony began, but the man held up his hand to stop the gunfighter from talking.

"We already know, señor."

Stony hung his head. "I am sorry for not speaking to you first."

The man with the deep but hoarse voice put a hand on Stony's shoulder.

"You honor me, señor, by coming to me now."

"I intend no dishonor to you or your family. I cannot explain what has happened to me — and to her. I adore your daughter and will treat her with only respect."

The Cantina owner studied Stony for a moment before he said, "It is called *relámpago en un arco iris* — lighting in a rainbow. Unexpected — and amazing. I saw it in her eyes. Teresa is like her mother. She is passion and fire like — *estrella cruzando el cielo* — how you say — a star — streaking across the sky. She chooses her own path and lights her own way." The 40-year old paused and then said, "Gracias for. coming to me."

"I had to, señor. An honest man could do no less."

"Then, I am pleased — for you and for my daughter."

That night The Silver Dollar was busy and hummed with rough cowboy laughter and a fair-sized crowd enjoyed their drinks. Two cowboys were climbing the stairs to the upstairs rooms with two saloon girls when Stony came in. Men were playing cards, but the most significant game was at the bottom of the stairs with Sloan Rush. This was a bigger stakes game than the others.

Stony found an empty place at the far end of the bar and ordered a beer. He drank alone, sipping his brew and only occasionally speaking to anyone. He stood there and had about a beer per hour for four hours. By that time, the crowd had withered, and only a pair of men sat with Rush at his table. By the look of him, one was a professional gambler, and the other was a traveling salesman. The bar owner claimed the last pot, and both the salesman and the gambler gathered their remaining chips, finished their drinks, and left the table.

Only then did Stony cross to Sloan Rush, who took a sip of a whisky he wasn't finished with.

"Is your working day over?" Stony asked.

Rush considered Stony a moment before nodding.

Stony pulled out the chair the salesman had used and sat. "Can we talk?"

Rush lit a cigar and took a deep pull before he spoke.

"What did Philomena have to say?"

Stony was a little surprised that Rush was aware of his trip.

"She told me you mentioned Crystal once that

she recalls. One drunken night when you were cursing her and almost out of your mind."

"Philomena has a good memory."

"Will you please tell me about my sister?"

"Mister, as I told you before, I don't know you."

"How do we fix that?"

"Perhaps you stay around a while — let me get to know you. I know you killed Silent March and that you've asked everybody in town about Crystal. That's not enough."

"What do you want to know?"

"Nothing from you. I'll find out what kind of man you are on my own. Maybe then I'll talk to you — maybe not."

The batwing doors slammed open, and heavy boot steps crossed the room to where Stony sat with Sloan Rush.

It was Elsworth Whittenburg — the broad-shouldered, jowly faced and deep-set eyed leader of the Whittenburg faction. He wore the same wide striped broadcloth vest and a cross draw pistol. He had two men with him, but his youngest son, Wylie, was not there.

"Stony Diamond," the man said, "I hear you done us a favor."

"Not that I'm aware of," Stony said, getting to his feet.

"Didn't you shoot Silent March?"

"Not for you. He was trying to kill me. And I didn't want to kill him — but he'd have it no other way."

"Don't matter. He was part of the Crenshaws, and you got him out of the way. We ain't forgettin' that."

"I told you on the street I want nothing to do with your feud. My killing of March wasn't for you. Don't count it as a favor. It wasn't."

"Have it your way, gunfighter. But I don't see why you're taking this the wrong way. March was a Crenshaw, and that's all that matters to us."

"If it had been one of your people who tried to ambush me — I'd have done the same thing."

"Don't go gettin' me pissed off."

"Then don't go getting me mixed up in your fight. It's not mine, and I don't want anything to do with it."

Elsworth looked at the two men with him.

"You try to be nice to some people, and it just don't work." Turning back to Stony, Elsworth said, "All right then. You didn't do us any favor — and we don't owe you a thing."

"Suits me," Stony said.

Elsworth told his men, "Get yourselves a drink, and we'll head back to the ranch. This was a waste of time."

The three men crossed to the bar.

"There," Sloan Rush said. "Now I know you a little better. Not enough — but some. Hang around a while. I hear you have a reason to with Alonso Huerta's daughter."

"She has nothing to do with the questions I'm asking."

"That's right. I'm not saying she does. She's a nice girl. Let's see how you treat her."

Stony clenched his jaw to keep his anger inside. He turned and left The Silver Dollar.

Santos Narváez was a known Mexican pistolero. He adorned his brawny body in a highly decorated and intricately stitched purple gaucho jacket, flared pants, and matching sombrero with a ruffled white shirt. He wore a pair of shiny Colt .44 pistols in concho adorned black holsters. He rode his high stepping palomino through Ciudad Acuña and then across the shallow flowing Rio Bravo into Del Rio.

His arrival in town spread like a lightning strike.

Stony was eating his lunch in the hotel when Narváez rode in. He knew what this meant. He put down his fork, wiped his mouth with his napkin, left money, including a generous tip, on the table, and walked out of the hotel.

Narváez rode the length Arteaga Street, the main street in Del Rio, and turned back to ride it again. This time he called out "Stony Diamond!" When he saw the black-suited man in the frock coat and Stetson, Narváez knew he had found his man.

The pistolero tied up his horse halfway back down the street and dismounted.

"You are not a coward, Señor Diamond. This pleases me. You will die an honorable death like a man — like el toro in the ring. They will write songs about this moment — corridos — to be sung for years to come."

Stony had pulled back his coat with his left hand from behind his back, ready to draw.

"Won't they be like all the other songs about the brave Mexican and the gringo?"

"Perhaps — but what else can I do, señor?"

"What if this story ends differently?"

"By your killing me?" The Mexican gunman laughed. "I don't think so."

"No," Stony said after giving the man a moment. "What if this were a story about the gringo who was afraid to fight the great Santos Narváez?"

"No, no. That could not be proven."

"What if you had my pistol to prove it?"

"Your pistol, señor?"

"What if I laid it in the dirt before you? You would have it to prove you were correct. Wouldn't that make for a better song and story?"

Narváez considered the idea for a moment and nodded his head. "That would be better. But how do I know this is not a trick?"

"Put your hand on your pistol. If I make any move, you question, draw, and kill me."

The pistolero liked this idea. He put his hand on his .44, and Stony walked forward. Using only his index finger and his thumb, he slowly lifted his Smith and Wesson American from his holster and dropped it into the dirt in front of Narváez. Stony released his coat with his left hand as he stepped back, but he kept his hand behind his back.

Narváez picked up the pistol while keeping his gun hand on his weapon and his eyes on Stony. When he had the American in his hand, the Mexican nodded and grinned.

"This is much better, señor. Now I don't have to kill you — and you get to live. But I'm afraid you will be known as a coward."

"I can live with that," Stony said.

"Muchas gracias, señor."

Narváez stuck Stony's pistol in his pants, mounted his palomino, and pranced out of town and across the river.

Teresa ran across the street from the cantina and threw her arms around Stony's neck. When she had held him a moment, she pulled back and looked him in the eyes asking, "Were you afraid of him?"

Stony smiled and said, "What do you think, Teresa?"

He pulled his second shorter pistol from behind his belt, and she looked down and saw it.

"Why?" she asked.

"Should I kill someone just because I can?"

She stood up straight and up on her toes and kissed him.

"You don't care what others will say?"

"It's only important what I know. And you," he said.

But Sloan Rush had seen Stony show his shortened pistol to Teresa.

CHAPTER 13

The incident between Stony and Santos Narváez occurred between the funerals for Fayette Whittenburg and Rowdy Crenshaw. Both were held at the Catholic church — Whittenburg at 10 in the morning and Crenshaw at 3 in the afternoon. Benedick Lattimer, the owner of the General Store, mayor, and part-time protestant preacher, conducted both services.

Stony attended neither, but after Teresa left him, he went to the gunsmith.

Dexter Ailes had Stony's Sharps rifle ready. The 46-year-old Del Rio gunsmith was chunky with slightly protruding eyes. He wore his sideburns long and had rough, calloused hands.

"I don't believe for a moment that you couldn't have taken that greaser som'bitch," Ailes said.

Stony didn't reply but produced his backup revolver and put it down on Ailes' counter.

"You know people in town are calling you, yeller?"

"If I am — it's something I'll have to live with. No one else."

The gunsmith waited a moment before he hefted the weapon. "What did you cut off — 4 inches of this barrel?"

"Three and three quarters," Stony said. "Can you cut and even 3 inches off this one?" Stony pointed to a nickel-plated S&W .44 American on display under glass."

"Yes. Do you want the site?"

"That would be nice."

"Tomorrow, good for you."

"Suits me fine."

The gunsmith lifted Stony's Sharps from behind the counter. "This one's ready to go."

Stony checked over the oiled and polished rifle. Ailes put a box of brass jacketed .45 - 70s on the counter. Stony selected one and leavened the breach block open. He inserted the metal cartridge and closed the block. He lifted the rifle to his shoulder and aimed out the front window. After a few moments, he eased the hammer down and worked the lever several times extracting the car-tridge and replacing it with another. Each time the action was smooth. Stony smiled.

"You do good work, Mr. Ailes."

"Thank you." He put the fringed saddle scab-bard on the counter. "Will two boxes of shells, do you?"

"Three, I think," Stony said.

Ailes stacked the boxes on the counter as Stony sleeved the rifle and paid the man for his work.

"Tomorrow?" Stony asked.

"Could be as late as the end of the day today, if you're in a rush."

"Take your time. Tomorrow's soon enough."

"I'll see you then," the gunsmith said.

Stony picked up his backup pistol and slipped it in his right-hand holster.

※

Back in his hotel room Stony was surprised by the light tap on his door. He put his hand on his re-volver as he opened the door to find Teresa Huerta holding a picnic basket.

"Lunch?" Stony asked with a smile.

"How about a ride out of town? All these fu-nerals today are depressing. And nobody is coming to the cantina to eat."

"Wonderful."

At the livery, Virg saddled a dark bay for Teresa and Stony took care of getting his flacon chestnut ready.

They road Northwest out of Del Rio to a stand of Live Oak along a clear stream.

As they ate, Teresa said, "My papa likes you. What did you say to him?"

"I was going to ask him for permission to court you — but he already knew we are — together."

"I told Mama. I couldn't help it."

"Does she know how much older than you I am?"

"Yes. I told her that, too."

"And?"

"She understood. She told me to be sure. And I am." Teresa leaned over and kissed Stony.

"Do you want to marry a gunfighter, Teresa?" he asked.

She looked at him for several moments.

"I never expected you to ask me."

"Did you want us to just be — lovers? What about children?"

"I cannot have children," she said hanging her head. "I was kicked by a wild donkey a few years ago. I no longe have — I do not have the problems other girls and women have each month. Doc Negrete told me I would not be able to have children."

"Then you do not want to get married?"

"I do, *mi amor,* — but I didn't think any man would want me."

"Now you know that is wrong. I want to ask your father if I can ask you to marry me, Teresa? What would you say to that?"

"*Si* — yes — yes!"

They made love again.

⊛

That Friday's Del Rio Post had the broad headline, "LOCAL FEUD EXPLODES." The story detailed the gunfight at Red House. It also rehashed the Dogleg Canyon fight and other killings that stemmed from the feud over a single calf. The attempted assignation of Stony Diamond was covered in its own story, as promised. The editorial of the week stated that the two families, the Crenshaws and the Whittenburgs, were disgracing themselves and hurting the town of Del Rio. Without taking sides, Tate Maxon put down in print that both families' acts brought shame on the town and the good people who were trying to make homes there.

A different story in the same edition told of the

Santos Narváez - Stony Diamond confrontation. As Tate wrote it, the showdown between the Mexican pistolero and the Texas Shootist could have been another killing. But instead, it ended with Narváez going back to Mexico without firing a shot.

The papers were sold out by noon, and in every saloon, shop, and Red House, the people of Del Rio absorbed the words of Tate Maxon.

After the service and burial of Rowdy Crenshaw, Theo Crenshaw was given a copy of The Del Rio Post. The 50-year-old had a slightly protruding stomach between his suspenders' arms, which strained to keep his pants up. He had an upsidedown U-shaped mustache under his nose and down to his chin. As he walked down the street from the cemetery, the Crenshaw leader's leader read the words in the paper. At one point, he stopped to reread some of what had been written. Suddenly he wadded the paper up and threw it in the dirt.

"This damn town!" Theo bellowed. "They don't like us here. Well, we don't like them either!"

The part-time preacher, Benedick Lattimer, caught up with the Crenshaws and heard Theo's words. He reacted as the town's mayor.

"What's going on, Mr. Crenshaw?" the 39-year-old storekeeper had a pockmarked face and sharp cheekbones.

"I just read your paper? You town folk don't like us, ranchers, much, do you? You sure like our money but not us."

"Is that what Tate Maxon is saying? He's one man. He doesn't speak for the whole town."

"Then maybe we should pay him a visit," Theo said, looking around at the other men with him.

His wife, Geraldine Crenshaw, 49, was a compact woman with a generous figure and soft face. Her redlined eyes held her husband's gaze as she stopped and pulled her arm from his.

"What are they saying, Theo? That we and Whittenburgs act like animals?"

He looked down at his wife of 34 years.

"Hasn't there been enough sadness today?" she went on. "We just buried another of your sons — another of *my* sons. If you do anything to make this day worse than it is, don't you *ever* come to my bed for comfort again as long as you live."

Theo took several deep breaths and put his wife's arm back in his.

"There will be a time," he said. "Not today — but it's coming."

CHAPTER 14

The Del Rio Town Council met in The Silver Dollar at 9 AM on Saturday. The Mayor, Benedick Lattimer, chaired the Council. The other members were gunsmith Dexter Ailes, Alonso Huerta, owner of the cantina, Tate Maxon, editor of the Del Rio Post, Doc Enrique Negrete, Sloan Rush, and, unofficial member, Leola Kensler.

"It was your editorial that got him riled up," Mayor Lattimer all but shouted at Tate Maxon across a cleared table.

"I was neutral in that editorial. I made a point of it. What did I say that was wrong?"

"That both families were bringing shame upon themselves and the town," Lattimer shot back.

"Is there anyone here who disagrees with that?" the editor asked.

No one responded.

"The point is," the Mayor finally said, "the Crenshaws think the town is against them. By now, I'm sure Elsworth Whittenburg feels the same way. The question is, what are we going to do about it?"

"Why isn't Sheriff Nils Glasford here," Doc Negrete asked. "He's a lawman."

"He is responsible for the whole county," the gunsmith said. "We're just a small part of that. You know how much time he spends out of town."

"Then that's the answer," Leola Kensler said. "We hire a Town Marshal."

"Like who?" Tate Maxon wanted to know.

"Stony Diamond," Sloan Rush said calmly.

"Diamond?" Leola asked, shaking her head. "I heard he turned yellow in front of Santos Narváez."

"Yes," several members of the Council agreed.

"Did he?" Sloan asked, twirling a poker chip between his fingers. "How many of you saw it?"

Only Alonso Huerta and Benedick Lattimer raised their hands.

"What did you see — exactly!"

The Mayor sat up, saying, "He dropped his pistol in the dirt in front of Narváez! He gave up!"

"Did he?" Sloan asked unruffled. "Is it possible

he did what needed to be done to keep from having a killing in our streets? The cost of a pistol isn't a very high price, I'd say."

"I did see him take on young Wylie Whittenburg. It was the fastest draw I've ever seen," Tate said.

"It was in front of my office," Doc Negrete said. "I could not believe it."

"Is there anyone at this table — or anyone you know who would go up against Stony Diamond? He has a reputation, and it's not as a coward."

The members of the Council sat back and digested this thought.

"Why would he take on such a job?" the gunsmith asked.

"I happen to know he has plans to say around a while — if we make it worth his while," Sloan said, giving nothing more away. "I think he'd take on the job. However, we need to understand that we're not talking about a $50-a-month cowhand with a badge."

"I've already made it a rule that no hardware is allowed in Red House," Leola said. "Why not make that the law in town?"

"Could we even get away with that?" Lattimer asked.

"Wouldn't that be up to a Town Marshal?" Sloan asked. "Which we don't even have yet."

"We make the laws for Del Rio," the Mayor said. "If we make it a law — and hire a Town Marshal — he would have to be willing to enforce it."

"Are we going to make such a law?" Sloan asked.

"If we make that kind of law, it would kill business." The Mayor suddenly switched to his view as a businessman. "Too many people carry pistols like they carry a pocket watch."

"I agree with that," the gunsmith agreed.

"Then let's focus on the question of a Town Marshal," Sloan said.

A silence settled over the meeting. It was newspaper editor Tate Maxon who finally spoke.

"I believe we can all agree on that. And, if he'd accept it, I think Stony Diamond would be the right person to approach about taking on such a task. My question is, how would we pay for it — and how much would it cost us? I, for one, am not making the kind of money Red House brings in each month."

"Let me talk to the other saloon owners," Sloan said. "I would be willing to ante up — say, $50 a month. I'm sure some of the others could do the same. Some less. And you, Leola?"

"I'd match that $50," Leola said without hesitation.

"We could get the other business owners to

contribute what they feel it's worth to them," Sloan said.

"All right," the Mayor said, "I can afford $35 a month — make it $40."

"I could handle $20," Dexter Ailes, the gunsmith said.

"Señor Huerta," the Mayor asked. "Doc Negrete?"

"Twenty dollars," the owner of the cantina said.

"The same," the town's doctor agreed."

"Put the Post down for $25 a month," Tate Maxon said.

"I believe we could come pretty close to $300 a month," Sloan said. "Maybe more. Let's say we offer $300 for a man to put his life on the line for us — and if there turns out to be more money collected, it could become the town's funds. You want to be our banker, Mayor?" Sloan asked.

"I don't mind collecting the money, but I would want someone else to keep the books, so there's no question about what we have and what we're paying." He turned to the newspaper editor, "Tate, would you be willing to do that?"

"Yes," but where do we keep the funds?"

"How about in my safe?" the gunsmith spoke up.

"I believe we have an agreement," Sloan said, looking around the table.

All the members of the Council nodded their heads.

"Who wants to be the one to ask, Señor Diamond?" Teresa's father, Alonso Huerta, asked.

"I'm willing to do that," Sloan Rush said.

"Then meeting adjourned," Benedick Lattimer said.

❦

Stony met Teresa's mother, Ofelia when he saw her father, Alonso and asked if he could marry their daughter. Ofelia was a good 15 years younger than her 48-year-husband. The lady had the blue-black hair of her daughter and a soft smile that swept up to her sparkling eyes.

Alonso spoke to his wife about the reason for Stony's visit. The lady's smile faded as she said something to her husband. He nodded his head and the smile returned.

"Ofelia wanted to be sure you understood about Teresa. That she cannot have children."

"She told me," Stony said and nodded to Alonso and to his wife he said, "Si, Señora."

Stony was welcomed with a hug from Teresa's mother.

CHAPTER 15

While the Town Council was meeting, Stony was out practicing with the modified pistol and Sharps from Dexter Ailes. The sidearm handled well and was close to being an exact replacement for the one Stony had thrown down in front of Santos Narváez. The action was easy, and he could quickly replace the cylinders. He spent an hour drawing and firing both of his pistols.

He paced out 800 yards and spent a half-hour using two boxes of shells to zero in the sights of the Sharps. In the end, he was pleased with both weapons. He cleaned and oiled them both thoroughly as well as the replacing cylinders before he reloaded them all.

Stony returned his horse to the livery and headed for the hotel.

Leaning against the hitching rail with his arms crossed was a waiting teenage gunfighter. Stony knew the look. The kid wore a fancy gun rig and had a cockiness about him that showed simply by the way he stood even with his arms crossed, and his hat tipped down over his eyes.

The young man pushed up his hat as Stony approached.

"You Stony Diamond — the coward Stony Diamond?"

Stony stopped.

"How old are you, kid?"

"Seventeen," the angular gunman bragged. He had a flat nose in the middle of an elongated face. His body was bony and lithe.

"Is this as old as you ever want to be?"

"You can't scare me. Any man who would throw down his gun to a Mexican is ready to die. I came here to take care of that little job."

"Got a name?"

"Why do you care? You won't live long enough to ever say it."

"It should be on your marker. Or it will read, 'Unknown.'"

The kid laughed. "Well, you sound sure, I'll say that for you. Obie Talver. You should know who it is that kills you."

"Talver. T-a-l-v-e-r?" Stony asked, working his left hand around his back and tugging his frock coat out from over his holster. "It should be spelled correctly."

The kid laughed and jerked his left-handed revolver.

Stony slammed two .44 slugs into the youngster's chest as Talver's barrel cleared his holster. The kid's 1858 Remington cap and ball pistol was cocked but never fired as Talver's body slumped into the dirt. The expression on the young man's face was surprise and terror. He was dead as he hit the ground.

Stony talked to Sheriff about the young gunman, Obie Talver. Undertaker Toot Ensley took charge of the kid's body and Stony supplied his age and name. Then Stony had lunch at the hotel.

People looked at him differently as the story of the gunfight in front of the hotel spread through town. Stony went to The Silver Dollar for a beer. Sloan Rush approached Stony at the bar.

"Should we expect more gunmen like the one this morning?"

"It's not my call. I did all I could to keep it from happening — but the kid was determined."

"Aren't they always?" Rush said. Then after a few moments of silence Sloan Rush said, "I have a proposition for you."

"I'm listening," Stony said, turning sideways to face Rush.

"We had a Town Council meeting this morning." Stony didn't respond. A silence hung between the two men until Rush went on. "There's a belief that we need a Town Marshal."

"Why is that? Sheriff Glasford seems to me that have a good handle on the law."

"He does. But there is a suspicion that the Crenshaws and the Whittenburgs could bring their feud to town."

"For what reason?"

"The same lack of common sense that produces feuds. Each side wants to do damage and spread anguish where ever possible. I think Theo Crenshaw took exception to something in Tate Maxon's editorial yesterday."

"How about the Whittenburgs?"

"No one has heard anything from them — but there is a suspicion that Elsworth and clan will be needled, too."

"And how is a Town Marshal supposed to solve that problem?"

"That will be up to whoever wears the badge."

"And if it comes to a gunfight?"

"The town has not and will not take sides in this feud. If the Crenshaws and the Wittenburgs bring their quarrel to town, there is a strong feeling that the citizens will take up arms behind the right man."

"So, you're asking me to be that man?"

"The pay's $300 a month."

Stony was surprised. He had been wondering what he could do to remain in Del Rio for the sake of Teresa. Was this the answer? How about his search for his sister?

"What are the options and limitations? Is there a set of town laws?"

"We don't even have a lawyer around here. Whatever the Marshal says, will be the law."

Stony turned over in his mind the possibilities and problems with this position.

"What about my encounter with Santos Narváez?" Stony asked. "Surely, there has to be some question about my abilities after that."

"No one got killed. That's what they realized."

Once more, there was silence between the two men.

"Who has the final say on this?" Stony asked.

"You do. The blacksmith, Felix Fernandez, is making a badge right now. If you accept the job, I'll get it for you."

Stony turned back to the bar and finished his beer. After he set the empty mug down, he said to Rush, "I'll do it. But I want to put a limit on when both factions can be in town. Two days a week each. Crenshaws on Mondays and Wednesdays — Wittenburgs on Thursdays and Fridays. Beyond those days, no more than 3 men from either side would be allowed in town — to visits to saloons and Red House."

"And how'd you enforce it?"

"I'll need 2 deputies — one at each end of town."

"How much would they cost?"

"For men, I could count on — let's say $150 a month."

"The total's more than the council agreed on."

"Those are my terms. Oh, and build a jail."

"Couldn't you share with the Sheriff?"

"I could, but if your Town Council is serious, this is what it will take."

"I will talk to them — but I'll take it on myself to accept on their behalf. Rush offered his hand, and Stony accepted.

Stony went to The Del Rio Post and ordered posters with his Crenshaw/Whittenburg restrictions on it. Tate took the order and their printer, Jaime, began setting up the order.

"You're billing this to the town?" Alvira Maxon asked. She and her husband, Tate, exchanged looks.

"Of course," Tate said.

"How long before they're ready?" Stony asked.

"Since you only want a baker's dozen, about an hour," Alvira answered.

"Then I'll come back for them."

Outside the newspaper office, Stony saw Sloan Rush walking his way from the blacksmith shop down by the river.

"Here's your badge," Sloan said, handing the nickel-plated star mounted over a brass circle. The words "Town Marshal" were stamped into the middle of the star and "Del Rio" at the top of the ring, and "Texas" at the bottom.

Stony pinned it on his coat breast pocket, saying, "Good. I'm going to talk to the lookout at The Empire. A deputy's pay is much better than he's making now. "

"Bailey Bowman. Good man. He'll likely take you up on the offer."

"Anyone else, you could suggest?"

"Santiago Jasso at The Shamrock. He's a bartender, but I've seen him handle a gun. And he's got sand."

"I'll go check him out."

By the time Stony came back to pick up the newspaper posters, he had two men with him.

Bailey Bowman was barrel-chested and preferred a coach double barrel .10 gauge. He had a jutting chin and a prominent brow ridge. In his middle 30's with chin whiskers and unruly eyebrows, he was not a man to be taken lightly.

Beside him, about the same age, Santiago Jasso stood in a faded blue shirt and two pistols, each on its own belt and holster. The revolvers were reversed in the holsters. He was muscular with wide-set dark eyes and a thick mustache. The Mexican was slightly shorter than Bowman, but both men had an air about them that exuded toughness and authority.

Tate Maxon handed the posters to Stony, who pulled two out and divided the others into equal stacks for each man.

"Get some nails from Lattimer's General Store and tell him to charge it to me. Nail these up around town. Particularly put them up so anyone entering town will see them. But pick up your badges from Felix Fernandez and then go to work."

Stony picked up the two posters he'd separated out. "I'm going to deliver one to both the Crenshaws and the Whittenburgs — personally."

CHAPTER 16

Stony's first stop was the Crenshaw ranch. He rode into the ranch yard without asking permission. He did not dismount but called, "Theo Crenshaw!!"

Three ranch hands to stepped out of the barn. A moment later, the head of the Crenshaw faction stepped out on his front porch. Crenshaw sneered through his U-shaped, downturned mustache. He focused in on the badge Stony wore.

"What's that you're wearin'?"

"My badge. Del Rio Town Marshal."

"There's no such thing."

"As of today, there is." Stony handed one of the posters he carried.

Crenshaw reached up, took the paper, and read

it. When he looked back up at Stony, the rancher's face was red and the veins in his neck budged.

"You're posting us out of town?"

"Only when the Whittenburgs are in town. You both get two days a week to do your business. And a couple of men a day can come in for the saloons and Red House and the like."

"You can't do this?"

"It's done."

"How do you plan to enforce it?"

"That's my job. Mine and my deputies."

"Deputies?"

"Crenshaw, you made a threat on the town. That's not the behavior of a good citizen. Until you can learn to behave yourself — you and the Whittenburgs — this is the way it's going to be."

Theo Crenshaw tore up the poster. "We'll see about this!"

"Yes," Stony said, "— we will. Don't be pig-headed and stupid. We both know the whole feud is getting people killed — and there's no reason for it."

"You said your piece — Marshal," Theo said. "Now, get off my ranch!"

Mrs. Geraldine Crenshaw was standing behind her husband just inside the door to the ranch house.

"How about Sundays?" she asked.

"Ma'am," Stony tipped his hat to her. "Most of the businesses are closed."

"There's church," she said.

"It's important to her," Theo said with a little less edge to his voice than before.

"Goin' to church is not a problem." Stony turned his horse, and rode away.

※

At the Whittenburg ranch, Stony received a slightly different from the reaction than at the Crenshaw's. Forty-six-year-old Elsworth Whittenburg stood on his porch looking at the poster. The broad-shouldered, jowly faced man with deep-set eyes was more surprised than angry at first.

"What brought this on?"

"Theo Crenshaw threatened to attack the town."

"We didn't."

"No, you didn't — and nobody's saying you did. But you know how little it would take for a full-scale war to break out on Arteaga Street. The wrong word, the wrong look from one of your hands or his — a lot of innocent people could get hurt."

Elsworth thought it over and showed the poster

to his wife, Blynn, a slender woman about her husband's age. She had a cleft chin, a widow's peak, and thick ash brown hair pulled back with combs. She wrinkled her forehead as she read the poster.

"Mrs. Elsworth," Stony said, tipping his hat to the lady.

"Okay," Elsworth said, "we can live with this. Two days a week — we should be able to do our town business with that."

"And Sunday's?" Mrs. Elsworth asked. "I'd like to go to church."

"Mrs. Crenshaw said the same thing," Stony said.

"Blynn's going to church no matter what you say," Elsworth said.

"Sundays are open — so — I'm hoping there's no problem there."

"How long do you figure this will go on?"

"As long as the feud goes on."

"Then you need to understand — Marshal — we will not be driven off our land.

"I wouldn't expect you to be," Stony said. "Nobody's happy with this — including the people in town — but it's the best way I can think of to keep things from blowing up."

"You may be right," Elsworth said. "But I've never seen this thing ending well."

"Good day," Stony said, tipping his hat and leaving."

⊱✦⊰

Deputy Bailey Bowman had a shaded perch under a pair of live oak trees at the North end of town. He sat on top of an upended wooden barrel in the bed of an empty wagon with his .10 gauge across his lip. The position gave him a good view a mile up the road.

Stony's other deputy, Santiago Jasso, leaned against a post outside the blacksmith's forge, looking out across the river. He acknowledged Stony's return but kept focused on his job.

Stony left his horse at the livery and walked to the Sheriff's office.

Sheriff Nils Glasford sat at his desk when Stony entered.

"Come in, Marshal," Glasford said cheerfully. "Take your hat off and make yourself at home." The 60-year-old had his feet up on his desk.

"You don't mind sharing your office until the town can build its own space?

"Not at all. It'll be good to have some company in here without someone being behind bars." Glasford's drooping mustache and a slash of beard from his lower lip down past this chin made him look a little like a fancy gambler. He was finishing up the job of cleaning his revolver and returned it to his cross-draw holster on his right hip.

Stony pulled up a chair from the table across the room near the potbellied stove. As he sat, the Sheriff picked up one of the posters Stony's deputies had nailed up around town.

"This seems like a good idea — if it can hold."

"It was the only thing I could think of to keep the Crenshaws and the Whittenburgs apart."

"Bailey Bowman told me you took one out to each side. How did that go?"

"Crenshaw tore it up, but Elsworth Whittenburg seemed to be all right with the idea — for the moment."

"Whittenburg may be younger than Crenshaw, but sometimes he has a cooler head."

"He said he won't be driven off his land."

"I've been through a couple of feuds in my time," Glasford said. "The two things I've learned is they all start over something not worth the trouble and the last well beyond when both sides should have let it go. Some folks seem to need someone to hate."

"Tate Maxon offered to buy a cow, a steer — I'll bet even a bull — if that would settle it. It wasn't enough for Crenshaw. He seems to want more blood."

"He does. And he'll get it unless I miss my guess."

"Do you think it will come to town?"

"It's the only neutral place between them — and eventually they'll want the town to take sides, or they'll try to burn it to the ground."

"After Rowdy and Fayette killed each other, I was afraid that was going to blow the lid off of it. I'm glad it didn't."

"According to Tate, Theo Crenshaw was ready, but his wife was all that held him back."

"I think Geraldine Crenshaw and Blynn Whittenburg have suffered the most in all of this," the Sheriff said. "I hope they live through it. If anything happens to either one of them, I'll hold myself partly responsible."

"Was there a time or a way you could have stopped this?"

"Oh, no. Feuds seem to have their own bile and their own heat." Sheriff Glasford shook his head and sighed before he said, "If you're going to be the law in this town, you need to know what no one is going to tell you. This feud has nothing to do with cattle."

"Tell me."

CHAPTER 17

Sheriff Glasford got up, freshened his coffee, and poured a cup for Stony. The Sheriff walked over to his barred windows and looked out into the street. He removed his hat and ran a hand through his thinning hair, seeing not the town but looking back into time.

"You remember the kid who took Silent March's horse from me at the Crenshaw's?"

"About 19, wasn't he?"

"Yup. Arley's his name. The youngest of Theo and Geraldine's boys. He has — had — a twin brother — Cleatus. They were both in love with Gale Whittenburg — 16. She kept playing them off against each other — teasing them — leading them on." The Sheriff paused in his story and shook his head and took a sip of his coffee. "It was too much for Cleatus. He hung himself on a tree where he used to meet with Gale and Arley."

Sheriff Glasford returned to his desk and sat in his chair.

"Nobody could find Theo — until someone decided to look in at Red House. He was supposed to be off buying cattle. But Theo was on a bender with Leola Kensler. It took an hour or so to sober him up before he could understand what had happened. By the time he got back to his ranch, Toot Ensley had already laid the boy out in a coffin on the dining room table. Theo smelled like a broken bottle of whiskey and sex when he walked in. I was there."

Stony tried to picture the scene.

"But that wasn't the end of it. Father Ochoa wouldn't let them bury Cleatus in the church's cemetery because he had killed himself." Glasford tightened his jaw against the memory of it. "And then there was Gale. She realized what she had done — and she lost her mind. She's withering away upstairs in the Whittenburg's house."

"Doc Negrete couldn't do anything for her," Stony said, filling in the next part of the story.

"Nobody could. She's starving herself to death, I think."

"I assume this happened before Tate and Alvira Maxon came to town and started their paper?"

"Yup. It's like a town secret. Nobody who knows it all will talk about it. This whole business about a stolen calf — it was just an excuse for the two families to go at each other. I don't see it ending. It could go on to the next generation — after Theo and Geraldine — and Elsworth and Blynn are gone. It might even last after both Gale and Arley are dead. I've seen it happen."

After some silence, the Sheriff added, "You know the frame going up for the church?"

"Yes."

"Most of that money came from Leola."

"They'll never let her in the church," Stony said.

"Oh, she knows that. And she knows she had nothing to do with the twins and Gale — but guilt over this whole thing runs deep. I think even Sloan Rush feels it, too. And he has nothing at all to do with it. But he closes The Silver Dollar every Sunday and stands outside to make sure no one bothers the services Benedick Lattimer and that congregation holds there."

"What do you know about Rush?"

"Not a thing. He and Myrta showed up here one day, and soon after, he bought what's now The Silver Dollar."

"Who is Myrta? She that scrawny teenage girl I've seen cleaning the tables?"

"That's her. Rush's daughter, we believe — although neither he nor the child ever says a word about their relationship or her mother. I'm not even sure they're related. Everybody thinks they are — but nobody asks. All anybody know for sure is that she doesn't work upstairs like the saloon girls. Will she one day? Who knows?"

Stony went to Our Lady Of Sorrows and found Father Ochoa working in his garden behind the church. For a man in his late 60s, the priest moved with seemingly little of the discomforts of his age. His craggy features were smiling when he recognized Stony. He put his rake aside and offered his hand.

"Marshal," he said, the pleasure in seeing Stony went all the way to his deep hazel eyes.

"Father," Stony said, returning, taking the priest's hand and smiling himself.

"I heard we had a new lawman, and I was pleased to see it was you."

This surprised Stony.

"Despite all the stories?"

"A priest hears many things, my son. Too much, sometimes, I think. I've learned to trust my fading eyes and my judgment over talk. Have you made any progress searching for your sister?"

"Some," Stony said. "But that's not why I'm here. You know I've asked Teresa Huerta to marry me."

"I do."

"And that I have the blessing of both of her parents?"

"I would expect that. But you are here because you wish me to marry you?"

"That is her wish and that of her parents. But you know..."

Father Ochoa put a finger to Stony's lips before the Town Marshal could complete his sentence.

"There are things it is better that I do not know for certain, my son. The church has many, many rules. I have found that I have, at times, done more hurt in my lifetime than help by following all of them to the letter." He looked out over the concentrated ground of the Catholic cemetery beyond the garden. "These days I regret some of my actions and our rules — but at the time, I thought I was doing what was right. Perhaps I am committing a sin of omission, even now, but I believe you to be a good Christian — for all that I know about you. I will perform the holy sacrament of marriage for you and Teresa. You will have my blessing — and, in my heart, I believe, that of the church. Let us speak of it no more."

Stony understood and nodded his head.

CHAPTER 18

The days passed with a new routine in Del Rio. The Crenshaws and the Whittenburgs kept to their allotted days. Both deputies kept to their posts, with Stony relieving them for lunch each day.

Stony made the rounds of the saloons, Red House, and the other businesses making a point to show up in places where a spark could ignite trouble. Everything ran smoothly.

The Town Marshal began having breakfast in a tented cafe, lunch in the hotel, after his deputies had eaten theirs, and had supper in the cantina. Everyone seemed to be happy for Teresa and him at their approaching big day. For the sake of propriety, they made a point of not making love any-more until they were legally man and wife.

Their wedding day was going to be the next Saturday, and the whole town was invited. Alonso and Ofelia were planning a bountiful fandango after the ceremony that would fill a block each way down Arteaga Street from the church.

Even Stony felt a little extra excitement every-where. Every time he kissed his bride-to-be, he had to work to keep to their agreement. He wanted her in every way possible, and she showed that she felt the same way.

Stony stopped into The Silver Dollar on a slow Friday afternoon. He ordered a beer from Diego, the bartender. When Sloan Rush approached him, Stony said, "Sorry for the downturn in your business."

"It was to be expected."

Traveling salesmen, cattlemen, and a few ranch hands from outlying ranches made up most of the 10 customers in the bar. Stony watched as skinny Myrta cleaned a table two salesmen left as they de-parted the bar.

"May I ask you something?" Stony asked.

"As long as it's not about Crystal," Rush said.

"It's not. Myrta. Is she your daughter?"

"She is — and I'll kill the man who says she's not."

"No offense," Stony said. "Simply wanted to know if she was kin to you — or one of the girls," he said, meaning one of the soiled doves that worked for the bar.

"She is my daughter," Rush said, forcing himself to suppress his anger.

"So, she'll one day own The Silver Dollar."

It took a moment for the saloon owner to answer, but he finally said, "I am hoping for something more for her."

"Since there's not a school in town, I assume you're teaching her."

"I am — and a poor teacher I am."

"The Catholic children go to school and Father Ochoa teaches them. But the protestants didn't want their children — indoctrinated."

"You are a protestant?"

"Let's just say, I'm not a Catholic."

"Perhaps if this feud cools down, we can get another school started in town."

Rush regarded Stony before he said, "You'll not be needing a school for any family of your own for several years. Why the interest?"

The idea that Teresa could not have children was not known to anyone beyond her, her parents and Stony. The idea that he would not have children caused the Marshal to pause, but he kept a poker face as he said, "If I'm a proper public servant — which I'm trying to be — it's a need I've come to be aware of, that's all. There are other children in town. I'm sure their parents have thought about it, too."

"And who would be the teacher?"

"The widow Fales might. I understand she used to be a teacher before she married, and her husband died. I'll wager she's tired of running her tent cafe. She could sell it — and perhaps she would be interested."

"Mrs. Fales. I would never have thought about her." Rush turned around and looked at his bar.

"Among the children in town, there are three at Red House. And the mayor has a son about ready to start school. With you, Lattimer, and Leola — I'll bet we could raise the money. It might even bring in some of the children from the ranches."

"I'm not sure how the town would feel about the children from Red House going to school with the others?"

"Ask the other parents when they chose their parents? When did they decide how their mother and father would make a living? The children at Red House had no say in their parents or their mother's work — just like every other child in town."

"You can be pretty persuasive when you want to be, Marshal."

"I'm only saying what is true."

"And a school would be a way to bridge the feud," Rush said, picking up on Stony's thinking.

"Well, it's something to think about."

Stony drank his beer.

Rush was looking a Myrta when he said, "I don't want her growing up thinking she has to go to work with Lollie and Rhea." The pair of working girls were laughing and drinking with a cattleman and a drummer across the room.

"She likely spends more time with them day to day than with you," Stony said.

Rush frowned at that thought.

"Most towns use their church as a schoolhouse during the week."

Sloan Rush smiled before he said, "That has always been the plan here.

"Oh," Stony said, finishing off his beer. "Guess I should have figured that."

"Still, it's good to know you're thinking along those lines," Rush said as he pushed off the bar and headed toward his table to go to work.

The day of Teresa and Stony's wedding was an exciting one for Del Rio. Our Lady of Sorrows was packed, and the couple was showered with rice as they came out of the church. It was just sundown, and the heat of the day was fading. A mariachi band had come from across the river in Ciudad Acuña. They struck up after the leader gave a thrilling Mexican outcry called a Grito. In moments the lawn in front of the church and the street was throbbing with music, singing, yelling, and even a few gunshots fired into the air.

The street was closed off for a banquet where Stony and Teresa had the center seats of honor. Stony's best man, Sheriff Glasford, offered a toast to happiness, long life, and many children. People were eating, dancing, drinking, and celebrating under strung rows of colorful Mexican fiesta paper lanterns.

Even the working girls like Lollie and Rhea from The Silver Dollar, other soiled doves from the different saloons attended alongside Delfina, Annetta, and Leola Kensler from Red House. Teresa's mother, Ofelia Huerta, made sure everyone in town was included in the celebration.

Around midnight, Stony and Teresa snuck away to the hotel. They had been given the most extensive suite looking out on the balcony for their wedding night. But as they approached the hotel,

Stony saw a familiar palomino tied up to a hitching rail in front of the hotel. Sitting in a rocking chair was the Mexican pistolero, Santos Narváez. He stood and removed his sombrero.

"Señor Diamond — or should I say, Marshal Diamond? Word has reached me that you are doing very well — that you even killed a gringo pistolero. I had to come see for myself. Good evening, Señora Diamond. Congratulations."

"What do you want, Narváez?" Stony said, moving Teresa to one side.

"Tonight — nothing, señor. It is your wedding night. I am not a man who would want to ruin that." The man's face lost its false humor as he said, "Tomorrow — I think we must finish what we started before." He reached into his sash and pulled out the pistol Stony had thrown in the dirt at the Mexican's feet. "Your pistol, señor. You will need this tomorrow. But tonight — I wish you a wonderful wedding night."

Narváez turned and walked into the night.

CHAPTER 19

Teresa had asked no questions as she and Stony went to their room. Inside together, he closed and locked the door. He turned and slipped his arms around her waist. She stared into his eyes as the fandango continued outside in the street.

"I am not scared," she said. "Should I be?"

"No," Stony said, kissing her lightly on the lips.

"Is this a thing I should expect in the future?"

"I wish I could say, 'No,' but the truth is there will always be those who want to make a name for themselves by being known as the man who killed Stony Diamond. Like that kid last week — most will be young — and nothing I can say or do will convince them they are about to die. When you are young, you can't imagine any future without you in it."

"But Santos Narváez is not young."

"There will be a few like him, too, I'm afraid. And there will also be men like Silent March — and other back shooters. We should have talked about this before. I am sorry, but that is a part of my life — and always will be, I'm afraid. Is it more than you bargained for?"

Teresa held her arms around his neck and slowly shook her head.

"I know you are a good and honorable man. I could not ask for more in a husband. You wear a badge, and you stand for the law. I am proud of that."

"I may not always be a lawman, my love. If — and when — the feud between the Crenshaws and the Whittenburgs is over — and it will be — someday — someday soon I hope — the town will not want to pay me what they are now. I don't want to be rich — but there will come a time when someone else can do this job, and I — we — will have to move on."

"Move on?"

"This can always be our home — but I will be called to other places — to help other people. If you do not want to come with me, you can stay here, and I will return when I can. I will always come back to you."

"And Santos Narváez?"

"That is a problem for tomorrow. Tonight is our wedding night."

Slowly a smile came to her lips, and they kissed — lovingly and then lustfully."

❦

Teresa and Stony were awakened to the mariachi band's trumpet and rousing sounds welcoming the new day. The newlyweds were ready to make love again when Teresa pulled away with a sheepish grin.

"We must go out," she told him.

"Why?"

"This is their call to us. It is tradition."

Stony sighed and gave his bride a peck as he got out of bed and dressed. He noticed that Teresa wrapped herself in their top sheet and picked up the empty wine bottle they had shared during the night. She was turning it over until a few drops of dark red wine splashed onto the bottom sheet. He questioned her with a look.

"You must take this out and hang it over the balcony."

Stony thought for a second and realized what these spots were supposed to be.

"Tradition," he said.

She grinned at him.

Stony stepped into his boots and buttoned his shirt before pulling the bottom sheet off. They opened the French doors to the balcony and stepped out with the sheet in his left hand, his right arm about Teresa, who proudly came with him to the railing in only the top sheet. He released her and spread out the bottom sheet to display over the rail. As the townspeople cheered, Stony lifted his bride in his arms and carried her back inside.

As Stony surveyed the crowd, he took note of Teresa's parents beaming as they hugged each other.

But off by himself, beyond the crowd, Santos Narváez leaned against the church with his sombrero tilted down over his eyes.

Stony and Teresa stood together a few minutes as the band played, and the people of Del Rio cheered. Then he took the sheet off the rail and gathered his bride to him as they went back inside.

As he closed the curtained door, Teresa said, "I saw him."

"I did, too," Stony said as he spread the sheet back on the bed. "But he'll just have to wait." He collected her into his arms, and she let the sheet fall to the floor.

It was late morning before Stony emerged from the hotel. He wore his suit coat, guns, and his badge. His eyes went to Narváez, who had parked himself against a hitching rail. He was spinning, twisting, tossing, and catching his shiny Colt pistols for the young boys gathered around him.

When Stony stepped into the street, parents rushed forward and snatched their children away. Narváez spun his revolvers into his holsters and walked out to face Stony.

"Must we do this here?" Stony asked.

"Of course, señor. I want it to be seen and for everyone to know that Santos Narváez cannot be fooled."

"No one tried to fool you."

"Ah, but you did, señor. You were not afraid of me. Perhaps now that you have a wife, you have something to lose. You should be afraid."

"Is that what you want? People to fear you?"

"But, of course." Then Narváez's expression changed as a new realization struck him. "You are not afraid."

"No," Stony said.

"You never were."

"I didn't want another killing in the street — for no good reason."

"But there is a good reason. I must prove I am better — faster — and more to be feared than Marshal Stony Diamond."

"I do not want to be feared," Stony told the gunman.

"You won't be," Narváez laughed an ugly laugh, "— at least not much longer."

Stony slipped his left hand behind his back and tugged his coat back from his holster on his right hip. As he positioned his coat in the middle of his back, he slipped three fingers of his left hand around the grip of his back up pistol in the tilted holster.

"The honor is yours, señor. You may draw first."

"I'm not going to start this," Stony said. "I don't want to kill you — remember that."

Narváez laughed again and flinched as he seized both of his Colts.

Stony moved faster than any eye could see. Those watching would later say his S&W seemed to appear in his hand suddenly. His revolver stabbed fire, and he produced his other pistol, which appeared to fire only a fraction of a second later.

Both slugs pounded into the Mexican pistolero's chest, one through his breast bone and the second an inch to it's right.

Narváez's weapons were both cocked and coming up level when the man was staggered backward, unable to find the strength to depress the hair triggers of either pistol. He felt himself knocked off his boots and hammered to the dirt.

The bright sun hurt his eyes until a shadow covered him and Narváez blinked. What had happened? He was looking up. Had he been beaten? Was he dying? It felt like it. He felt his pistols drop from his hands, and he couldn't get his breath. There was a coppery taste of blood in his mouth. And the brightness was fading, fading, and then there was nothing.

In the bedroom on the second floor, Teresa had watched the gunfight and found she had not been filled with fear. Instead, she crossed herself and said a prayer for Santos Narváez.

CHAPTER 20

Santiago Jasso came running at the sound of gunshots. The Mexican deputy was still wrapped in his sarape from having kept to his post through the night. He arrived at Narváez's body with both of his pistols out and ready to do battle.

Stony looked up at Jasso, who said, "I thought he was a mariachi. He didn't wear his guns when he came across the Rio on the ferry. Someone else came with his horse."

"It all belongs to the town, now," Stony said, replacing the spent shells in both his pistols.

A crowd started to gather.

Stony unbuckled Narváez's gunbelts and pulled them out from under the body, which rolled one way and then the other. The Town Marshal spun the two Colts' cylinders and collected the bullets in one of his coat pockets before putting them back in their holsters.

"I'll take the guns to Dexter Ailes — horse to the livery — and the saddle over to Edson McReary's. See if they think they can sell them for commission."

"You know Narváez's has a price on his head across the Rio." Deputy Jasso said. "I can drag his hide across and collect the bounty."

"Good idea," Stony said. "The money will go into the town coffers — help pay for you, Bowman, and me."

Jasso almost laughed but didn't. "I'll use my horse to carry him over. If I used his, they'd likely want to keep it."

Stony nodded his head.

Leading Narváez's palomino with the ornate silver cinched saddle up the street, Stony discovered his bride dressed and waiting for him on the porch of the hotel. He stopped long enough for a good long kiss and then went on about his business. She almost skipped across to the Cantina to see her parents.

Del Rio was quiet, and the separation of the feuding families by their time in town seemed to damp down that rage. There were stories that riders from both ranches had seen each other out on the range, but so far, nothing had occurred.

The next incident that demanded Stony's attention happened in The Silver Dollar.

A professional gambler named Dallas Cadwallader was the first customer of the day. He ordered a whiskey at the bar and went straight to Sloan Rush's table. He looked 40 and flabby, his skin had large pores, and he sported a full, wax curled mustache. He displayed a flashy stickpin in the purple silk ascot cravat he wore with a gray frock coat.

Sloan ordered the box of new cards from the bar, and Diego delivered, standing between Rush and Cadwallader. It took the gambler a few moments to select a deck. As he did with his left hand, he hung his right straight down by his chair.

Before Sloan could break the seal and get the selected deck out of its container, Myrta, who was sweeping the floor nearby, abruptly lifted her broom and slapped Cadwallader in the elbow.

"Don't you try to cheat my Pa!" she demanded.

In a reflex, the gambler backhanded the child as he stood and reached into a vest pocket from which he produced a Derringer. Myrta hit the floor, and Sloan snatched his short ivory-handled

Hopkins & Allen .36 caliber revolver from his shoulder holster. Before the gambler could aim, Sloan shot the man in the head. He fell across Myrta's feet.

By the time Stony got to the saloon, Myrta was sitting in her father's lap with her head on his shoulder and her arms around his neck. Sloan explained what had happened, and Stony picked up the cold deck Myrta had knocked out of Cadwallader's hand. The deck was not in a box. By holding it in his left hand and fanning the cards, Stony could tell that some cards had their edges shaved. He fanned them a second time and opened to a trimmed card to reveal it was a king. Stony dropped the deck on the table.

"Myrta," he said to the girl, "how are you doing?"

She sat up and looked at her father and then at Stony. "I'm okay," she said.

"Good," Stony said. "You are a brave girl to do what you did."

"I wasn't afraid. I knew Pa would protect me." She put her head back on Sloan's shoulder.

Stony picked up the .40 caliber single shot Derringer, broke it open, and dropped its unspent shell on the table.

Sloan Rush reached between himself and his daughter and pulled out his .36. He placed it down on the table. Stony picked up the revolver and examined it before returning it to Rush.

"I'll get Toot to pick up the body," the Marshal said.

Myrta turned toward Stony. She said, "Are you really my uncle?"

Stony looked at Sloan and back to Myrta. "I think so — but your father isn't so sure."

She looked at her father and said, "I hope he is, Pa."

CHAPTER 21

Benedick Lattimer's General Store was directly opposite Our Lady of Sorrows and opened both on Artega, the main street, and Magnolia the cross street. Folding doors rolled back to a post at the corner of the structure on the boardwalk 6 feet back from the streets. Each morning Lattimer pushed displays of fresh foods to the boundary of his property.

Theo Crenshaw was shopping with his wife and foreman in Lattimer's when he spotted the Town Marshal sitting on a bench on the boardwalk across Artega. Crenshaw stormed across the street toward Stony.

"I don't like you watching us!" the steely-eyed ranch owner began yelling as he walked through the dust. His slightly protruding stomach led the way, and the man wasn't threatening to Stony, which angered the rancher even more.

Upon the boardwalk where Stony sat, Crenshaw bellowed through his upside-down U-shaped mustache.

"This is our day in down."

"It is," Stony agreed.

"We ain't doin' nothin' wrong."

"Did anyone say you were?"

"Then why are you sittin' here watching' us?"

"Two reasons. One, it's part of my job. And, two, I'm here to make sure the Whittenburgs don't show up and start something."

"We don't need your protection!"

"You never know. Wouldn't you hate it if someone raced through town on a horse firing wildly and happen to hit one of your people — maybe your wife, for example?"

"I'd kill anyone who even tried such a thing."

"And rightfully so. But you are standing over at Lattimer's shopping with your back to the street. If someone were to come racing down the street, I'll bet I'd see them before you would."

The logic of Stony's proposition angered Crenshaw as much as anything else the Marshal might have said. When Theo couldn't come up with a retort, he asked," Do you do this when the Whittenburg's are in town?"

"I do. I can be found right here most Mondays, Tuesdays, Wednesdays, and Thursdays — exactly like I am today."

Finally, in undeniable frustration, Crenshaw wheeled around and stomped back to the General Store.

⚜

Teresa joined Stony for lunch in the hotel dining room. He had already relieved both of his deputies, and they had returned to their posts. It was the last day the newlyweds were supposed to stay in the honeymoon suite, but Stony had extended their stay until the end of the month.

Spread across the table under their lunch dishes were three sheets of clean newspaper print Stony had obtained from The Post. It was the sketches and plans for the house Stony, and his bride were building a block away on Flores Street.

The house was going to be adobe with two-foot thick walls. A half dozen workers were already busy making the clay and straw bricks on the site Stony had purchased. Another group was framing the house, awaiting the sun-dried bricks. This second group was making arched doorways and windows.

"Have you ordered the furniture from Lattimer's?" Stony asked.

"No. I have an uncle and some cousins across the river who make wonderful beds, chests, tables, and chairs. I've told them what I want," Teresa beamed.

"How about curtains?"

"Lattimer's does have cloth for that. Mama will help me make them."

Stony made some marks in the blocked out stable behind the house.

"What's that?" Teresa asked.

"We'll need a place to keep grain and a closet for the tack."

"Oh," she smiled.

A rider raced by the hotel, and Stony jumped to his feet and ran outside.

❧

A few moments before the rider, a Whittenburg ranch hand, had been stopped by Deputy Bailey Bowman at the North end of town. Bowman has his .10 gauge up to his shoulder, ready to fire with the rider pulled his lathered horse to a hard stop.

"This ain't the Whittenburg's day in town," Bowman said.

The rider, a rangy young man in a well worn

and faded red shirt and chaps, held up his hands. "It ain't fer me! Doc Negrete is needed out at the ranch! Right now!"

"Take off your gun," the Deputy demanded.

The cowboy quickly complied, hanging his gunbelt over the edge of the wagon.

"Go ahead on, then," Bowman said.

The young cowboy kicked his horse back into a full gallop. He flashed past the hotel and leaped down at the Consultorio Mèdco. Out of breath, the young man ran into the building.

"Doc. It's Gale. They think she's dyin'!"

The short herbalist with a receding chin and broad nose grabbed a burlap sack with an assortment of instruments, bottled plants, and cures. He hurried outside with the cowboy.

"I'll have to get my horse at the livery," Doc Negrete said.

"No time. Take mine," the young rider said, grabbing the reins of his horse and handing them to the doctor.

The doctor swung into the saddle and retreated up the road the way cowboy had come.

"It's a Whittenburg!" Rufus Crenshaw shouted. The second youngest son, who had lead Dogleg Canyon misadventure, pulled his revolver as he approached.

Others of the clan began to arrive, including Theo. But Stony arrived at about the same time.

"Whatever you're doing, stop!" Stony yelled, pulling one of his pistols. He quickly stepped between the winded cowboy and red-faced Rufus. "What's going on here?"

"There aren't supposed to be any Wittenburgs in town today," Rufus said cocking his revolver.

Over his shoulder, Stony asked the rider, "Why are you here?"

"Doc was needed out at the ranch. They sent me to get him. They think Miss Gale is dyin'."

"Put your gun away," Stony ordered.

"No way," Rufus said.

"Do it," Theo said, pushing his way through the crowd.

Rufus eyed his father and reluctantly did what he was commanded to do.

"I thought you were on duty looking out for us?" Theo spat at Stony.

"What would you do if someone needed Doc Negrete in a hurry at your ranch, and it was the Whittenburg's day in town?"

Theo had no answer for that.

"Everyone cool down," Stony said as Deputy Bowman approached, holding the double-barrel shotgun across his chest with both hands. He had the rider's gunbelt thrown across his shoulder.

"He's breaking the law," Theo said. "What are you goin' to do about it?"

"I'll take care of him," Stony said, reaching out to his Deputy for the gunbelt. Bowman handed the leather and pistol to the Town Marshal. "The rest of you go on about your business."

The gathered crowd broke up and drifted off.

"You come with me," Stony said to the cowboy.

"What did I do wrong?"

"Not a thing. But until Doc Negrete comes back, you've got no horse. We'll have some coffee at the Sheriff's office while we wait."

CHAPTER 22

Gail Whittenburg's death was reported in a special edition of The Del Rio Post due to a lengthy illness. The funeral mass was set for Friday. No Whittenburg made an appearance in town on their assigned Thursday, but no one was surprised.

Stony felt tension in the air. There had been no confrontations between the two feuding sides, but even Sheriff Nils Glasford could feel it when he returned from checking on some missing cattle at one of the smaller ranches out in the county.

"What's going on?" Tate Maxon, the newspaper editor, asked the two lawmen mid-afternoon Thursday as the two rested on the Sheriff's office's porch.

"You tell us," the Sheriff said. "You're the one with his ear to the ground."

"Everything I know is in print," said the stocky man in his usual bowler hat and neatly trimmed beard and mustache. "It's like a lull before a storm. But I can't figure out where the storm's coming from."

"Neither can we," Stony said, scanning the street in both directions.

"I can tell you this," Tate said, "every gun in town is loaded and within reach."

"That include The Post?"

"You bet. We've always had a pistol in the office and a rifle in the corner. And if it comes to it, Alvira's a better shot than I am. Even Jaime carries a knife with him — and it's not for typesetting."

"When I rode in, Virg told me all the horses in the livery are acting strange." Sheriff Glasford said.

"I haven't seen any of the girls from Red House out and about. Isn't this the time of day they do their shopping?" Tate asked.

"It is," Stony agreed, getting to his feet. "Think I'll take a turn around town. Anyone want to meet me for a beer at The Silver Dollar in about an hour?"

"I will if I finish my paperwork in time," the Sheriff said.

"Sorry," Tate said. "I've got to come up with

something to print for tomorrow's edition. Right now, it's pretty much a blank page — front and back."

⚜

Stony's first stop was Edson McReary's saddlery.

"Marshal," the gaunt leather artist said, looking up from a pair of boots he was working on. Edson was in his mid-30s, had a square jaw and long, calloused fingers. "I've had some lookers at the saddle, but no offers yet."

Santos Narváez's black saddle with silver ponchos and handworked leather pommel, fenders, and stirrup wings was on display in the saddlery's front window.

"Don't sell it cheap," Stony said.

"Oh, I won't," the craftsman assured the Marshal.

Edson got off his working stool and went into his back shop. He returned a moment later with a black shoulder holster rig.

"You're going to have to take your coat off, Marshal, and unbutton your vest to get this on."

Stony laid his coat across the counter and opened his vest. He turned around so Edson could help him slip the two and a half inch, smooth shoulder strap on his left shoulder. A separate half-inch wide strap with a buckle at on end hung from the holster..

"This goes under your vest, through the back, and you buckle it here on the front edge of the holster."

Stony worked the strap around him and backed out the left shoulder opening, where he tightened the belt and put the prong in the third hole of the leather. There was a loop on the holster's body where Stony threaded the extra length of the strap. He rebuttoned his vest.

Edson handed Stony the pistol he'd used as a guide. It was the new S&W American gunsmith Dexter Ailes had sold him and shortened the barrel. It fit into the holster perfectly with the pistol grip and trigger guard exposed. The sheath of leather was stiff and open down the front side while moulded to hold the weapon in place. Then Stony slipped back into his coat, and all evidence of the concealed weapon disappeared.

Stony tried pulling the pistol several times and was pleased with the ease it afforded.

"Edson, you're a master at your craft."

"Well, my Pa was a great teacher — and I work hard to do good work."

Stony paid the man half again as much as they'd agreed upon before Edson began work. The leather craftsman was surprised and looked up at Stony.

"Excellent work deserves excellent pay."

"Thank you, Marshal."

❦

Neither Sheriff Glasford nor Tate Maxon was at The Silver Dollar when Stony finished making his rounds of the town.

"Come sit down," Sloan Rush called.

"I've paid for my lessons," Stony said. "I've learned to keep my money and let you do your work without me."

Rush laughed and pushed out a chair to his right with his foot. He also stacked the cards off to his left. "I don't need your money."

Stony took his beer and joined the saloon owner at his table.

Without a preamble, Rush said, "I used to be an outlaw."

The remark caught Stony entirely by surprise. "Used to be?"

"And never in Texas. I used to rob trains and stagecoaches — companies but never passengers."

"Why'd you give it up?"

"Because Crystal asked me to."

This was the first time Rush had mentioned

Stony's sister since their first conversation months ago.

"I would have done anything for her. That's why I go to so much trouble to make sure people I gamble with know I'm not cheating. I've learned to read people, and that's what I do."

"Are you going to tell me about my sister now?"

A sadness came over Sloan Rush before he said, "She died. Died of consumption. She's buried in Waco."

"Why couldn't you tell me this in the first place?" Stony asked, his lips tight.

"Because she was a whore. Was — until I helped her leave all that behind her. She was the good woman you would hope your sister might be. But in her early years — she did what she had to do to survive. Can you understand that?"

Stony let out a breath as he relaxed his face. "Yes. I wouldn't hold it against her."

"She always wondered and worried about you. Leaving you at that orphanage was all she could do."

"I figured that," Stony said. "If I had ever found her, I would have made it, so she didn't have to work."

The two men sat in silence a minute before Stony asked, "Did she say anything about our parents?"

"Your father was a prizefighter. Pretty good at it from what I've learned over the years."

"Sheriff Glasford saw him fight once."

Again there was nothing for either of them to say until Stony asked, "How about Myrta? Is she my sister?"

"If you mean did Crystal love her — yes? Another girl was going to throw the baby away to die when Crystal took her. She grew up knowing Crystal as her mother and me as her father."

Stony thought this over and took another drink of his beer.

"If my sister loved her like a daughter, then I'm her uncle. You can tell her that."

Sloan nodded his head, looked down at the table a moment, then back up at Stony, saying, "There's one more thing."

"Whatever it is, say it."

"Crystal was your sister — but was also your mother — by your father."

CHAPTER 23

Teresa detected the change in Stony when he came for supper at The Cantina. She sat down at his usual table on the patio and reached for his hands.

"What is it?" she asked.

It was a long moment before he looked up into his bride's eyes.

"It's something we must talk about — tonight — later."

"I can take a few minutes now," she said.

"No," Stony breathed out and tried to smile. "But there is something I want you to do in the morning. Please come back after the funeral and stay close to your parents. Everyone feels it — I'm sure you do, too." He scratched an itch on the back of his neck. "Whatever it is that's coming — I don't want you in the hotel. The walls are too thin. If lead starts to fly, this is a better place to be."

"The feud?" she asked.

"I'm not sure. But it seems likely."

"Tomorrow?"

"That's what I'm thinking."

"But it is Gale's funeral."

"I know — but I'd feel better if you were here."

Teresa smiled, stood, and kissed Stony on the cheek. "Whatever you say, husband." She went to get his meal.

Hours later in their honeymoon hotel room at the Hollett House, Stony stood looking out across the balcony at the town, his Bible in his hand. Teresa was behind him adjusting the glow of the lamp on the dresser.

"What is it you need to tell me?" she asked.

Stony closed his eyes an instant as he turned around to face his bride, his Bible still in his hand. They stood in silence as a full minute passed. Finally, Stony said, "I found out this afternoon about my sister."

Teresa smiled, "Doesn't that please you? I thought that's what you wanted."

"I also learned — she is more than my sister."

"More?" Teresa didn't understand.

"She is also my mother."

This news was absorbed by Teresa but she didn't move.

"By my father," Stony added after a moment.

Teresa stepped up to her husband and placed a soft hand to his cheek. "What does this mean to you?" she asked.

Stony shook his head slowly saying, "I'm not sure. My father was a prizefighter and very quick with his hand. I am guessing that's where my speed came from."

"What else do you know?"

"Nothing."

"So you don't know if your sister — your mother — was forced or ...." She couldn't finish the thought.

"No. I guess I don't."

"You do know that she cared enough about you to see that you were well cared for in a place where you could grow up."

Stony sighed and sat down on the bed, closing his Bible and putting it on the bedside table.

"Yes, I know that."

"And she didn't want you to carry this burden."

"But I do. We covered this in seminary — and I've been reading and rereading for the last couple of hours."

"What have you learned?" Teresa asked in a hesitant voice.

"That I could be a *'mamzer'* — a bastard. That I *'shall not enter into the congregation of the Lord — even to my tenth generation.'* The sin is called *'Kareth'* — and the punishment is either dying young or dying without children — and that my soul could be *'cut off'* from the children of God."

Teresa sat down beside her husband and took his hands in hers.

"We already know we won't have any children," she said.

"Yes, and — supposedly this only applies to Jews."

She searched his eyes for understanding. "Do you feel you will die young?"

"No. Every man who faces me with a gun, I've always known I was faster than he was. Always."

"And you never kill anyone unless you have no choice."

"Yes." He studied Teresa's face, "But whatever this means, I did not want to hide it from you."

"The moment I first saw you, Stony Diamond, I knew I loved you — no matter what. I still do. And I always will."

"I felt the same," he said. "And *I* aways will."

"Do you feel you are doing what you've been called to do?"

"I do."

"Then remember, '*the Lord works in mysterious ways...*' and you are one of them."

She went to the lamp, turned it all the way down and blew out the flame. Teresa undressed in the moonlight coming through the window. When she was naked, she came to him and they made love.

CHAPTER 24

Gale Whittenburg's funeral mass was spoken in Our Lady of Sorrows by Father Ochoa. She was buried in the cemetery behind the church. Stony kept his distance but was at the edge of the crowd. He and Teresa were the last to offer their condolences to the girl's parents before leaving the gravesite.

Sloan Rush had closed The Silver Dollar and cleaned it for a wake following the service. Instead of heading for the celebration of Gale's life, the crowd held up in the churchyard.

As the crowd slowly came around the church, they discovered Theo Crenshaw standing with his Winchester on one hip and a burning torch in his hand. Blynn and Elsworth Whittenburg arrived in front of the church with Father Ochoa.

To Father Ochoa, Theo Crenshaw shouted, "You would not bury my son because he killed himself! Yet, you accept the girl who caused it all!"

In his black robes, Father Ochoa worked his way through the crowd to face Theo about 70 feet away. "Theo, what are you doing?"

"I'm going to burn this whole damn town to cinders!" He tossed his torch onto the boardwalk of Benedick Lattimer's General Store. The boards had been soaked with coal oil and burst into running flames.

Lattimer, who had closed his store and attended the service out of respect, ran forward, shouting, "Start a bucket brigade!"

Lucian Crenshaw, the Crenshaw nephew who had been wounded in the Dogleg Canyon incident, stood up on the hotel's roof. He raised his rifle and fired at Lattimer's feet, making the storekeeper stop.

"No, you don't!" Theo shouted. "Let it burn!"

Stony stepped away from Teresa and fired at the cowboy on the hotel roof. He didn't hit the shooter, but his shot must have buzzed by Lucin's head because the ranch hand ducked and jerked back.

Theo lowered his gun and fired at Father

Ochoa. The priest grabbed his side as he fell to the ground.

Stony fired at Theo, but the man was already on the run up the street.

More shots were heard down the street toward the Rio. Another Crenshaw fired at Stony from the alley beside the hotel. The crowd rushed for cover inside the church. Stony pushed Teresa behind him and put two shots into the board near the new shooter's head.

The Whittenburgs pulled their guns, and there was open warfare in the streets of Del Rio. Elsworth said to his youngest son, Wylie, "Protect your mother!"

Alonso Huerta, Teresa's father, made sure his wife and Teresa were safely inside the church before he rushed back outside. Stony had fanned shots up and down the street when his father-in-law hurried up behind him.

"Give me a gun!" Alonso shouted over the gunfire.

Stony saw who was asking, and he pulled his backup pistol from the holster in the rear of his belt. He gave it and a loaded cylinder from his gunbelt to Alonso. Without a word, Stony raced across to the hotel.

Up and down the street, Wittenburgs were firing at torch-carrying Chrenshaws.

Benedick Lattimer ran into his store and emerged from the smoke with two hands full of stacked buckets. He handed them to Tate Maxon, who quickly formed a bucket line. Lattimer was at the end of the line, splashing the filled containers onto the flames.

Doc Negrete helped Father Ochoa into the sanctuary and ripped open the priest's cassock to treat the wound.

Stony ran through the hotel and out the back door. He hurried toward the alley, ready to trap the second shooter. But there was no one there.

"Drop your gun!" came a call from behind Stony. He heard a pistol's hammer click back, ready to fire. Stony dropped his pistol and raised his hands to shoulder height.

"Turn around, Marshal. Very slowly. I won't shoot even you in the back. But "I am going to kill you.""

Stony eased around. When he was perpendicular to the man with the gun, Stony slipped his right hand inside his coat and pulled out his third pistol from his shoulder holster. As he continued to turn, he fired one shot and fanned another into the gunman, waiting with a pistol in his hand.

The man was Rufus Crenshaw. He was thrown back dead into the dirt.

A back door opened, and a woman with a rifle

stepped out down the back of the building. It was Alvira Maxon. She raised her rifle and fired at the shooter on the hotel roof. Lucian Crenshaw tumbled through the air, dropping his rifle beside him as he hit the ground.

Alvira raised a hand to Stony. "Jamie just nailed one with a torch out front!" He waved back at her. "Have you seen Tate?" she asked.

Stony picked up the pistol he'd thrown down and blew the dirt out of the cylinders before the called back, "He's helping put out the fire at Lattimer's."

"Good," she called. "If you see him tell him Jamie and I have got the paper covered."

"Will do!" Stony said as he headed back into the hotel.

Gunfights were happening up and down the street. Storekeepers, saloon owners, and barkeeps were battling to protect their property as Crenshaws and Wittenburgs threw shots at each other.

In his hotel room, Stony grabbed both his Winchester and his Sharps and stepped out on the balcony.

CHAPTER 25

Because the Wittenburgs were fighting the Crenshaws, the Whittenburgs were also fighting for the town. But none on either side were marksman, and few shots hit anything besides the fronts or side of buildings.

At the North end of town Deputy Bailey Bowman had been overpowered. Three men were tying his hands behind him while a forth readied a hangman's noose. The trio managed to get Bowman up on his horse while the other man tossed his finished loop over a limb.

They were 500 yards away when Stony propped his Sharps on the bottom slat of the rail surrounding the hotel balcony. He took very careful aim and shot the rope tosser in the chests. The hefty slug of the shot threw the hangman to the ground. The sound of the shot, which arrive a split second later, spooked the horse and the animal raced away. Bowman hunched over his saddle horn and worked his feet into the stirrups as he made his escape.

The three men helping with the hanging jerked around and tried to figure out where the shot that killed their partner had come. They crowded behind the empty wagon and threw wild shots down the street.

On the opposite end of the street gunsmith, Dexter Ailes, blew a Crenshaw off the boardwalk in front of the store with a Winchester round.

Deputy Santiago Jasso had both his pistols out and was firing at approaching cowboys.

Stony couldn't locate Theo Crenshaw. The clan leader was under the overhang in front of The Silver Dollar firing inside while he doused the door and boardwalk with coal oil. He lighted it before running away up the street under the shelter of other buildings.

The fire brigade had moved from Lattimer's General Store to Edson McReary's Saddlery. Gunfire from the Crenshaws quickly made them retreat.

Sheriff Nils Glasford had left town early that morning on another rustling call, or he would have been in the fight, too.

Alonso Huerta was looking for a target with Elsworth Whittenburg beside the church. Sully Crenshaw, who still walked with a limp from being wounded in the street the day Stony first arrived, fired as he crossed from behind a building. Sully fired again and hit Elsworth with his second shot. The rancher slammed back against the white walls and left a blood trail as he slid to the ground. Sully cocked and fired again at Alonso. The older man stepped out and walked straight at Sully, returning shot for shot. Alonso's fourth shot caught Sully in the stomach, and he froze where he stood. Alonso fired once more and hit Sully in the chest. He was dead before he could bite any dust.

Stony shot two more of the would-be hanging party with his sharps. He punched rounds through the side of the wagon where they hid. The remaining rider grabbed a horse and fled the town and the fight.

Arley Crenshaw, the one remaining twin, tried to pick up the can of coal oil a ranchhand had dropped when shot by the print setter at The Post. He grabbed the can and splashed in on the boardwalk but was shot through the glass panes of the front door by Alvira Maxon.

Theo crossed the street carrying his can of coal oil. Stony took a bead on him and shot. The can burst open, and the clan leader was soaked in the liquid. The shot tore through Theo's ribs. In fact, the round went all the way through his body. He was flung to the ground. The torch he carried ignited a trail of coal oil in the dirt right to Theo's body. Within moments he was a flaming corpse.

The front of The Silver Dollar was blazing. Two men from the brigade ran to the watering trough and began throwing water on the flames.

"Help!" the voice of Myrta came out of the saloon. "Pa's been shot!"

The men couldn't get inside until they reduced the flames. They kept pitching bucket after bucket of water.

Stony left his perch, rose, and hurried inside his hotel room, parking the Sharps against the wall but taking his Winchester with him.

By the time he got to The Silver Dollar, all the gunfire had stopped, and the streets were silent — except for the sounds of the bucket brigade. He ran to the saloon and dashed through the remaining flames to find Myrta holding Sloan Rush, who was bleeding from two shots in his torso.

Diego, the bartender, was wrapping his bloody arm in his apron as he sat on the floor in front of the bar. "I'm okay," he said.

Stony dropped to his knees beside Rush.

"Pa!" the girl screamed as Stony took the weight of the injured man's body onto his lap. "Do somethin'!"

Rush was able to open his eyes as his breath came in shallow gasps.

"Nothin' t' do, girl," he said. "Sorry for dying on you."

"Oh, Pa!" Myrta wailed.

"I wanted — to leave her — more than this place," Rush struggled to say.

"She's got a home with Teresa and me," Stony told the dying man. "I am her uncle."

"Thank — you," the saloon owner was slipping away.

"We will bury you next to Crystal," Stony said.

Rush looked into Stony's eyes, and a slight smile crept across his face until his eyes closed and he was gone."

Myrta threw herself across her father's body and wept.

Del Rio was a town in deep mourning. Toot Ensley, the undertaker, was exhausted trying to prepare the bodies for burial.

The next day, Benedick Lattimer presided over

all the protestant service which were held in The Silver Dollar. Toot Ensley's transported the bodies to the cemetery.

Father Ochoa was similarly occupied for the Catholics. The priest moved slowly and had a hard time getting his breath because of a broken rib. But he read mass for all the Catholic dead, both Whittenburgs and two Crenshaw ranch hands.

The last service Father Ochoa conducted was one day later, at 9 AM. It was a mass for Sloan Rush.

Several people in the community had kind words to say about the gambler and saloon owner because he had been such a good citizen for Del Rio. Nothing was said about Lollie and Rhea, the soiled doves Rush had employed, and who sat in the back of the church.

But Rush was not buried in the church cemetery but returned to the undertaker's. There the portly mortician spread salt over Rush's body. His casket was then placed in a larger, double-walled box that was packed with ice.

Following the service, Blynn Whittenburg and Geraldine Crenshaw met out in front of the church. Both ladies dressed in black. Young Wylie, the only remaining Whittenburg male, went to get the wagon for his mother.

Blynn spoke first, offering her hand to Geraldine.

"Geraldine, I'm so sorry — for everything."

It took a moment before Geraldine could speak. "I am, too, Blynn." She took Mrs. Whittenburg's hand.

"What are you going to do?"

"The only thing I can do is to go back to St. Jo. I still have family there."

"Are you going to sell your ranch?"

"Yes."

The two women stood looking at each other a moment before Blynn Wittenburg said. "I won't insult you by offering to buy your land."

"You're going to stay here?"

"So, yes, I'm staying. Because Wylie stayed with me, I still have one son left. And ranching is all I've ever known. I'm sorry you're going — but I understand." Geraldine nodded her head as Blynn went on, "As I was saying, I won't insult you by offering to buy your land. But let me say this — whoever you sell it to — if they try to get away with paying you less than what the land's worth, you can tell them you already have a cash offer for whatever you want. I'll back that up if push comes to shove. But I know you don't want to sell to any Whittenburg, and I don't blame you. But I won't let anyone rob you."

Tears flowed from Geraldine's eyes once more. "Why couldn't our husbands be like that?"

Blynn could only shake her head.

CHAPTER 26

Stony left Diego in charge of The Silver Dollar and said he would return to Del Rio after his mission to Waco. Teresa and Myrta sat on the wagon seat as Virg helped Stony tie the reins of three horses to the wagon's back.

Sheriff Nils Glasford returned just as Stony was ready to climb into the wagon seat at the livery.

"Who've you got there?" he asked, removing his hat as he stepped down from the saddle.

"Sloan Rush," Stony said.

"My Pa," Myrta said. "We're taking him to Waco and will bury him beside Ma."

The Sheriff nodded his head slowly. "This was a hell of a thing," he said, looking up and down the street at the charred buildings and black bunting and wreaths among many of the buildings. "I shouldn't have missed it."

"Don't know you could have made much of a difference," Stony said. "You would have had to shoot people you knew and maybe gotten shot yourself."

The Sheriff sighed rather than respond to Stony.

Stony took off his badge and handed it to Glasford. "Here, give this back to the Town Council. They don't need me anymore. Either Bowman or Jasso could do the job — if either one of them even wants it."

"You comin' back?" Glassford asked as he pocketed the star.

"Our house over on Flores will be finished by the time we get back," Teresa said. "And Myrta is going to live with us." She hugged the child, who forced a smile.

"Then, I'll see you when you get back." "Virg!" he called out the livery owner who had gone back inside.

The Sheriff pulled his horse to walk his horse around the wagon when a young gambler stepped out of the shadows from across the street. He had his pistol drawn and cocked in his left hand. "Hold it, Sheriff. Unbuckle your gunbelt and let it fall."

Glasford looked at Stony, who was trying to

place the gunman. The Sheriff raised his hand, holding his horse's reins, and unbuckled his belt with his other hand. His weapon dropped to the ground.

The man turned his attention to Stony.

"You don't even remember me do you?" He held up the right hand, which was missing a thumb. "I know you — Stony Diamond — and I'm going to kill you. Here and now."

"I don't even know your name," Stony said, turning to face the gunman.

"And you never will." The man raised his pistol a mite.

"I tried to help you," Stony said. "I could have killed you back in Junction. But I didn't."

"No, you shot off my thumb — made me a cripple. But you didn't know I'm as good with my left hand as I am with my right."

"And this is where you've decided to die?" Stony said sadly.

"Not me — you —. Good-bye."

"How did you even find me?" Stony asked quickly.

The gunman lowered his pistol slightly and laughed. "People like to tell stories about you. I liked the one about your turning yellow before that Mexican..."

Before the man could finish his thought,

Stony's pistol was in his hand, and a .44 slug stabbed through the air and hit the gunman square in the breast bone. Stony fanned another shot beside it, and the gunman's face was in shock. He was thrown backward and saw the sky darken as his open eyes were swept over with death.

Sheriff Glasford asked, "How did you do that? He had his gun ready to fire."

"But he wanted to talk. When men talk, their mind isn't on their hands. An d we're all slower than to react than to act."

Glasford leaned down and grabbed his revolver before stepping up to look down on the young gunslinger. Virg hurried out and froze when he saw the dead man. The Sheriff reached over and picked up the unfired gun in the dirt, easing the hammer down.

People hurried out to see what was happening.

The Sheriff started going through the man's pockets but, aside from a few dollars in the vest and some change in his pants, the lawman found nothing.

When he stood, Glasford said, "I guess he'll be another unknown."

"His name was Branch — Branch Quade," Virg said. "Least that's what he told me a few minutes ago when he left his horse with me."

"I'll see that's put on his marker," Glasford

said. He turned back to Stony, Teresa, and Myrta. "You folks go on if you hope to make Udvale by dark. I'll tend to this trash."

Stony ejected the spent cartridges from his pistol and replaced them both with fresh rounds from his gunbelt.

"Thanks, Nils," put a boot on the wheel hub and mounted the wagon seat. Stony took the wagon reins and popped them. The double team pulled out into the street.

Teresa, and Myrta had just witnessed a killing. They didn't, however, feel frightened. As the wagon started up, Teresa looped her arm in Stony's arm, and Myrta leaned over and pulled herself closer to them both. They felt very safe.

THE END

Thanks

Thank you for taking the time to read <u>Ode To An Outlaw</u>. I hope you enjoyed it. If you did, please consider posting a short review on line at the site where you purchased the book and telling your friends. Word of mouth is an author's best friend and much appreciated. I love to write these stories, but it's even better to sell some and to know other people take some joy from them, too.

If you're interested is subscribing to my monthly newsletter, contact me at jacks@ wrightbridgepress.com. You know when my next novel is coming out and a little bit about how I work. I would love to hear from you.

Thank you,
    Jack R. Stanley

ABOUT THE AUTHOR

Jack R. Stanley is an award winning novelist, playwright, and screenwriter. As an officer and combat photographer in Vietnam, he earned the Bronze Star. Yet he says, "When you're in a firefight and everybody else on both side have guns while you have a camera --- you get to change your pants a lot."

After his military service he received both his M.A. and his Ph.D. at the University of Michigan in Ann Arbor in Radio-TV-Film. His doctoral dissertation was on the long running TV series GUN-SMOKE. Stanley also received two of Michigan¹s most prestigious creative writing awards, The Hopwood Award, one for a one-act play and the second for a novel.

Still married to his gifted high school sweetheart, Stanley's first academic position was TV Area Head at The University of Texas at Austin's Department of Radio-TV-Film. He later moved to deep-south Texas and the Lower Rio Grande

Valley for a challenging position with The University of Texas-Pan American. Here he taught Theatre-TV-Film for 30 years in the Department of Communication serving as Department Chair at U.T.P.A. for 11 years. He did take one year out to work for The University of Alaska Anchorage as a visiting professor. Back in Texas, Stanley directed for stage at The University Theatre, produced and directed fifteen student staffed, cast, and crewed feature films, writing most of the original screenplays. Just a few of his credits are available on IMDB.com.

He now lives in the Texas Panhandle where he writes his fiction.

BONUS

Eight chapers of <u>Occurrence At Latigo</u>.

OCCURRENCE AT LATIGO

By

Jack R. Stanley

Occurrence at Latigo
Copyright © 2019 by Jack R. Stanley.
All rights reserved.

Credits:
Edited by
Mary Lee Stanley
and
Rose Marie Reed
ISBN: 978-1-947726-60-4
Wrightbridge Press

jacks@wrightbridgepress.com
www.thefictionwritersnotebook.com
www.jackrstanley.com

CHAPTER ONE

F ive rough looking riders approached a bluff in broken country. This was mostly prairie. There were a few trees and stands of boulders. High up in the rocks a western rattlesnake coiled itself back into a defensive circle. A large man's boot was nearby but motionless at that moment. The man, almost a mountain unto himself, covered by a buffalo robe, had worked his way up behind a large boulder overlooking the on-coming riders. This was Tarr Phillips. Sighting down on them with his Winchester, he froze at the sound of the snake's rattle. The venomous creature was coiled only inches away from him and ready to strike.

Phillips looked down on the serpent with irritation. In a lightening quick move, he pinned the snakes' head under his boot.

He turned back to the riders. The one in the lead rode a dun and had his sweat soaked hat with the brim flatten up again the crown. Phillips set his sights on the scruffy rider's head, knowing the bullet would drop on its path to its target over the distance. The big man in the rocks squeezed the trigger slowly until his weapon jerked in his hands.

The first rider was thrown from his saddle with the slug catching him in the center of his chest. The others instantly jumped from their saddles and sought cover behind their horses. They threw wild shots in the general direction of the bluff. But these were pistol rounds and none actually made the height and position of Phillips.

Phillips ducked out of sight and turned his attention to the snake wrapping itself around his boot. He calmly took the reptile by the head and looked into its threatening eyes. The rattler wrapped itself around his arm.

"You stupid critter," he said.

With a flick of his big arm, Phillips flung the snake away. Then he retraced his path back down the rocks to his horse. The reptile, which had landed in between some rocks, slithered away into the shadows.

Down below on the other side of the boulder,

the riders continued to shoot wildly. It was their leader, Gus Fry, who waved them off. Fry had a gut that over-topped his belt and he was as dirty as he was out of shape.

He had made it to cover behind a rusted iron colored rock. He peered out and studied the bluff they were approaching.

Unseen by Fry or this gang, Phillips returned his rifle to its scabbard and climbed into the saddle of his dapple gray. He rode on.

It would be a while before Fry and his men did the same.

꿍

Thunder rumbled not far away. It had rained recently and would again, soon. It was spring in the Texas Hill Country. A pair of good but not matched sorrels pulled a relatively new farm wagon. The ground was already near to being an ocean of mud and the animals had to struggle. Ahead was the one street town of Latigo.

A man and a woman were mounted atop the wagon seat. The man, in his early 30's, wore a poncho and a soaked hat. He had broad shoulders and was clean shaven. He drove the wagon with an attractive woman, five years younger and wrapped in a blanket beside him. This was Lyles and Sarah Quinn.

A group of men on the porch of the town's lone saloon watched the Quinn's arrival.

Luther Bobbs, a feisty ol' ranch hand of 40, sat on an empty keg, carving on a block of wood with his pocket knife, and spat into the street. Beside him stood Fenn Burch, 50's, an aproned barkeep with a soft belly. His blonde hair was thinning.

A 36 year-old cowboy with a splint on one leg, Dave Shambow, stood pissing into a puddle beside the saloon. He had a coffee cup in his free hand. His hair was long and greasy and his beard was scraggy with missing patches were no hair grew at all.

Shambow spoke as the wagon passed nodding his head in greeting, "Lovely day, ma'am."

Shambow was pleased with himself. Fenn, the barkeep, popped Shambow on the arm with his bar towel.

Sarah turned away in disgust. Quinn didn't see Shambow as he was focused on guiding the wagon on down the muddy street.

Quinn stopped at the depot/general store. He was a fit man and very agile. He climbed down and helped his wife to the boardwalk. She went in under the overhang and looked up at him.

Sarah, wringing out her long chestnut hair, said

to her husband, "If you say so much as one little word to me, Lyles Quinn, just one, that sounds like 'I told you so' — I'll kick you, so help me Hanna!"

Lyles couldn't help but grin. "I'm not saying a thing," he said suppressing a laugh on his blue eyed face.

But after another moment, they both burst into laughter as they embraced. They shared something very special. And the love between them was not difficult to see.

CHAPTER TWO

B ack on the porch of the saloon, Fenn, Bobbs, and Shambow watched the Quinns.

The lame cowboy buttoned up his pants as he said, "Dumb sod buster. Why in th' hell bring somethin' as nice as that out here?"

The barkeep said, "Careful, Shambow. She's his wife. Livin' t'gether is what married folk do."

Shambow shook his head, "Won't be but a couple a' years 'fore she's as used up and worthless as that ground he's pickin' at. I ain't sayin' I'd mind doin' some of th' usin'?"

The older ranch hand, Luther Bobbs looked up from where he sat carving and said, "Shambow, how can you stand t' eat with th' same hole you talk with?"

"What?" Shambow asked as if he'd said nothing they weren't all thinking.

"That mouth of yours is going to get you killed," Fenn said as he wiped his hands on his apron, shook his head and went inside his saloon.

The inside of the Elite Saloon revealed nothing like its name. The place was plain, drab and barely a functional saloon.

A young gunfighter, Willy Hyer, sat playing an endless game of solitaire. The kid wasn't old enough to shave. His attempt at a mustache was laughable. He wore his pistol low slung. His attempt at swagger was as threatening as his flat coal black eyes.

There was a stove in the center of the saloon. Two farmers sat near the stove. Ned Guthrie, a tired looking late 30's, always seemed to be angry at the world. He wore a threadbare jacket, torn jeans, and down-in-the-heel boots. Jess St. Clair, approaching 50, was a weather-beaten, stoop-shouldered man with a determined face half covered with a throat length beard.

The barkeep crossed by the farmers and said, "Quinn jest come in."

St. Clair, the older of the two farmers, stood and pulled on his wet boots which had been drying beside the stove. He reached for his coat. Guthrie stayed seated.

St. Clair asked, "Ned, you comin'?"

"Directly," Ned Guthrie said.

The other farmer indicated he hadn't finished his drink.

St. Clair walked out to the porch.

Fenn got behind the bar as Shambow limped in, giving a dirty look to both farmers before he crossed to the bar. He picked up his empty coffee cup and showed it to Fenn.

"Coffee's free," the barkeep said returning to the stove and reaching for his pot. "but I could run out almost any time now, Shambow."

St. Clair walked across the saloon turning up his collar and went outside.

Shambow held his empty coffee cup to Fenn.

Shambow said, "I'll buy some more bad whiskey — in a while."

Fenn poured Shambow a cup of coffee, "Bad is the onlyest kind I have."

"Okay, damnit, give me a glass of it."

Shambow tossed a coin on the bar.

Fenn sat up a glass for Shambow who held his nose and drank.

"Damn! This crap tastes like somethin' you just spit in, Fenn."

"For you, Shambow, I just might," Fenn said recorking the bottle. Shambow turned his back to the bar and picked up his coffee looking out the front doors. "One of these days I'd like t' grab me a hand full of that little gal."

The gunfighter looked up from his card game. Guthrie looked up at Shambow.

The sullen farmer said, "Who you talkin' about, Shambow?"

"That little gal your boy Quinn married. She is one fine lookin' piece a' woman."

The barkeep warned, "Shambow!"

"Shut up, Fenn. Even farmers know what happens 'tween a bull an' a heifer."

Guthrie examined his drink, gulped it down and stood. He noted Shambow's coffee cup in the lame cowpuncher's hands. Guthrie elbowed the hot contents onto Shambow's injured leg. Shambow yelped in pain.

As Guthrie strode toward the door, the young gunfighter stuck out a leg in the farmer's path.

"That's kind'a like back shootin', ain't it!" Hyer asked.

Guthrie realized what Hyer was saying. The farmer swallowed hard.

"Man's got no right t' talk that'a'way 'bout a good woman."

"As I understand it, she's a farmer's bitch."

Fenn leaned across the bar with a .12 gauge single barreled pump shotgun in his hands aimed directly at Hyer.

"Less you figure you're faster than double o buck, mister, don't even think about movin'."

"Say, friend, I don't like people wavin' guns in my direction.

Fenn said, "I ain't wavin'. I'm dead center of your gut."

Hyer took a breath but decided that's all the moving he was interested in doing.

To the farmer, Fenn said, "Get out of here, Guthrie!"

Guthrie stepped around Hyer's leg and left with a little quicker step than before.

To the kid, Fenn said, "If you want t' stay in my place, drink my bad whiskey, an keep on breathin', you get back t' your card game."

"I learned a long time ago not to cross the barkeep."

Hyer slid back under the table and picked up the deck of cards.

Fenn slowly lowered his shotgun and returned it to its place under the bar. He picked up a new bottle and crossed to Hyer's table where he poured the gunfighter a drink.

"On th' house." Fenn said.

CHAPTER THREE

O ver in the freight depot and general store, water still dripped from the edge of the roof. Lyles Quinn and Jess St. Clair stood talking at one end of the porch. Sarah was combing the water out of her hair at the other.

Trudging through the mud from the saloon, Ned Guthrie approached.

"Hello, Ned," Sarah said.

Guthrie tipped the brim of his partially dried hat, "Ma'am."

"Turned out to be a little wetter than I thought," she laughed. "Only fools and newcomers, right? I qualify as a newcomer."

"Yes, Ma'am," the farmer said. Ned wasn't

much for talking to women. It was one of the things he never got the hang of.

Guthrie walked over to the other men.

"If it was just me, Lyles, I'd say sure let's give it another year," St. Clair said. "But it ain't."

"I understand," Lyles said as he looked up to see Guthrie. "Ned."

"Lyles," Guthrie said.

"Jess here says he's not sure he wants to buy any more seed."

"Can't blame 'im, can you?"

"No," answered Quinn. "But we're having some good rains."

"You still goin'?" Guthrie asked.

"That's why I'm here — waiting on the stage."

Jess St. Clair asked, "Ned, you plannin' t' stick it out another year?"

Ned Guthrie looked like he was closer to quitting than continuing, but he said, "Might."

"That's the kind of talk I like to hear," Quinn said slapping Ned on the shoulder.

"I ain't said nothin' fer sure."

"Come on inside and let me show you something. It's a seed catalog. Sarah, you comin'?"

"In a minute," she said still combing the last of the rain out of her tresses.

Quinn stepped over and they exchanged a small kiss.

After Quinn and the others had gone and Sarah had returned to running a comb through her hair, she saw something in the distance.

A rider on an Appaloosa came out of the distance toward town. He smoked a pipe and wore buckskins and tall boots. His coat was a thigh length buckskin with some fringe.

At the Elite Saloon, Hyer came out on the porch. He didn't notice the rider but focused his attention on Sarah.

She saw Hyer and didn't like his look. She turned and went inside the depot.

Hyer looked away and up the street. He saw the rider. Luther Bobbs looked up from his carving. He gestured toward the man on the horse and spoke to the young gunman.

"That's th' man you need t' talk t' about a job, young fella. Names' Zeak Thorndyke. Biggest rancher in these parts."

"Looks t' me like he's some kind 'a squaw man."

"Was once. These days he could buy an' sell th' both of us 20 times an' never miss th' change."

Dave Shambow pushed past Bobbs and hobbled out. He saw Thorndyke coming, too.

"Oh, hell." the stove up cowboy said.

He tried to straighten up and walk to the far side of the porch where he tried to hide his splint from Thorndyke. Luther Bobbs spat and almost hit Shambow on the foot.

"I got kicked by a jackass once," the old cowboy said. "Up in Montana Territory. I was stove up all winter. Hadn't been fer that ol' jackass I'd of died fer sure."

He paused and chewed a moment before continuing, "Either you fellas ever had jackass steaks? How about jackass ribs? Damn! I sure do miss that ol' jackass sometimes."

Thorndyke rode up to the saloon. He was 46 and clean shaven. But the marks of a hard life showed on his lined face.

Shambow greeted the rider, "Zeak."

"Luther. Shambow."

Thorndyke saw the splint on Shambow's foot.

"How long you had that, Shambow?"

"Couple a weeks," the shabby ranch hand said. But he quickly added, "It's gettin' better."

Thorndyke frowned as he flipped his reins over the hitching post. As he loosened the Appaloosa's cinch, he said to Shambow, "Whose out at the line shack."

"Clovis."

"He doin' his work as well as yours?"

"We trade out. I jest come into town this morin'."

Inside the depot Guthrie produced a wad of rolled greenbacks. Reilly, the storekeeper, was behind the counter watching.

"There's thirty-two dollars here," Guthrie said. He handed the money to Quinn. "You best count it."

"Your word's good enough, Ned. If you say there's thirty-two dollars here — there's thirty-two dollars."

"Then I don't need no receipt. Jest give me your hand."

They shake hands.

"Thirty-two plus St. Clair's sixty-four, the Southwich's forty, the Ogan's twenty-seven plus Sarah and my fifty-six —I've got two-hundred-nineteen."

"You — you ain't carrin' a gun?" Guthrie asked.

"We don't own one — except for the rifle out at the place. I'm leaving that with Sarah."

"What you got there is 'bout all th' money I have in this world."

"It's also just about all the money we have in this world, too, Ned," Sarah said joining the conversation.

Guthrie pulled out a cap and ball pistol and handed it to Quinn.

St. Clair stepped up.

"You need a better gun than that." St. Clair said. "Here, Lyles. Use this." St. Clair produced a Remington 44. six shot cartridge revolver from the big pocket of his coat.

Quinn took the Remington and returned the ball pistol to Guthrie.

"How about a holster?" Reilly asked from behind the counter. He pulled up a used holster and belt. "This isn't fancy — or new — I took it in trade for somethin'. You can have it Quinn."

"Why would you give anything away?" Guthrie asked.

"I'm bettin' on you folks, too. If you stick an' do well — I'll do okay."

"I'll buy all the seed in a lot. Maybe we'll get a better deal," Quinn said slipping on the simple belt and holster. The .44 fit just fine. "Now, will you two see to it that Sarah gets home all right?"

"Of course," St. Clair said.

The sound of the stage coach arriving was heard. They all went outside.

CHAPTER FOUR

The stage driver climbed down. He was wrapped in a yellow slicker but soaked through. His drooping hat hung down on both sides of his face. He handed a mailbag to Reilly before he turned to see the group.

"If'n any of you plan t' ride with me — you'd best not be in any hurry. I ain't movin' till I'm wrung out, dried out and fed up!"

"Your supper's waitin'," Reilly said.

With that the driver slogged past the group and went inside.

"You fellas want t' check th' mail?" Reilly asked.

"Sure," St. Clair said.

The men followed Reilly inside.

Luther Bobbs had crossed from the saloon. He

stepped up on the porch behind Sarah.

"Ma'am," he said tipping his hat. "Thought you might like this."

He handed her the wooden horse he had just carved. It was still warm from his handling it.

Sarah was surprised as she examined the minutely detailed sculpture.

"This is lovely, Mr. Bobbs."

He didn't respond to her compliment but went to work changing the team of the stage.

❧

Thorndyke stood at the bar as Fenn finished pouring a drink.

"Stage's in," Fenn said. "This is th' third week you come in expectin' that Winchester. You sure it's comin'?"

Thorndyke swallowed his drink instead of answering.

The door opened and Hyer walked in and crossed to the bar.

"You, Zeak Thorndyke? Own a spread 'round here?"

Thorndyke eyed the young gunman.

"Who's askin'?"

"Name's Hyer. Willy Hyer. Ya' might a' heard a' me."

"Nope. What you fishin' for, boy? You know who I am."

"I hear you're short a line rider."

"What's that t' you?"

"I could use th' work."

Thorndyke looked Hyer over carefully.

"You don't look t' me like you've seen th' workin' side of th' sun in a coon's age."

Thorndyke reached out and took one of Hyer's hands and turned it palm up.

"Your hands been holdin' cards instead of rope an' pliers. My guess is you're better with a hand gun than you are with steers."

Hyer jerked his hand back.

"You sayin' I can't do th' job?"

"I ain't said I got a job."

"This time a' year you ain't gonna find many men lookin' fer work."

The rancher thought this over a moment.

"Can't do a thing for ya'."

"You're sayin' 'can't.' What ya' mean is 'won't.'"

"Young fella, Fenn tells me you already tried t' start a fight with a farmer."

Hyer threw a glance at Fenn who quickly busied himself.

"So? I got no love fer dirt eaters."

"They're here t' stay."

"I know some ranchers that b'lieve different."

"Twenty years ago the Comanches said th' same thing about ranchers. Lot of 'em died 'fore they got smart enough t' see it weren't no use. I don't plan t' make th' same mistake with farmers. I got no job for you."

Thorndyke finished his drink and walked out of the Elite Saloon. Hyer watched Thorndyke go with growing anger.

Luther Bobbs backed the fresh team into the stage traces. Quinn and Sarah were off by themselves. Quinn admired the wooden horse Sarah showed him while she read a letter.

"My sister's had her baby. A girl. She named her after Aunt Denise."

St. Clair and Guthrie stood a ways off minding their own business.

"I'm never going to like saying goodbye to you," Quinn said. "And I don't think I'll be very good at pretending I do."

"Then promise we won't do it much."

"Promise," he said putting his arms around her. "I'd feel a lot better if you would stay with the St. Claires."

"We settled that. I'm staying in my home -- our home. Maybe I'll finally be able to get some things done around there. All the things you haven't left me alone long enough to do," she said with a wink.

Quinn frowned. He didn't like to hear her joke about sex, at least not in public. She kissed his frown away.

"I'll miss you, Lyles."

"I miss you already."

Quinn released Sarah as he saw Thorndyke approach. Thorndyke tipped his hat to Sarah and nodded to Quinn. The buck-skinned clad rancher climbed up and looked on the top of the stage. Not finding what he was looking for he climbed down as the stage driver came out of the depot with a tooth pick in his mouth. He grinned.

"It's inside. On th' floor. Thought I'd try to keep it dry

Thorndyke opened the stage door and pulled out a long wooden box. He set his box down on some barrels by the depot. Thorndyke pried his box open with a Bowie knife from his belt. He pulled out a Winchester '73 rifle.

Luther Bobbs whistled.

"No wonder you been s' anxious. That's a beauty."

The Quinns, St. Clair and Guthrie also gathered around to admire the new rifle.

CHAPTER FIVE

H yer strode out of the saloon. He appeared with an angry expression. He saw the people over at the depot and he stepped out into the muddy street.

"Hey, Squaw man!" Hyer called.

Thorndyke slowly and methodically returned the rifle to the box before he turned to face Hyer.

Hyer started across toward Thorndyke who waited patiently.

The gunman spoke again, "I don't like askin'. But I'm goin' t' be real nice today an' ask you fer a job — one more time."

Thorndyke stepped into the mud, but there was no deadly snake-like slithering to his steps Hyer had.

"Is that what this is all about?" Thorndyke asked.

"Them your farmer friends there? I see th' *coffee coward* over there."

Guthrie swallowed hard and moved out of the way.

Quinn moved Sarah out of the way, ushering her toward the protection of the building.

Thorndyke faced Hyer in the street.

"I never did like boot lickers or sod busters," Hyer continued his taunt. "My ol' man was a sod buster. He weren't worth a damn." He took a breath before he said, "Now how about that job?"

"I got no need for a gunfighter."

"That's goin' t' be jest too damn bad. 'Cause I got no use for a squaw man."

Quinn felt the revolver in his belt but he didn't like the thought of using it. He looked around for an alternative and saw something.

Hyer moved around and Thorndyke countered him stepping away from the stage.

"You can even make th' first move, squaw man."

"I got no reason t' draw on you."

"Well, I'm goin'a kill ya, if'n you draw first or not. It don't make me no never mind."

The two men continued to move around staying opposite of each other. Hyer stopped when he neared the depot. The sun had come out and was then in Thorndyke's face. The rancher allowed his hand to drop slowly toward his revolver.

Quinn reached into one on the wooden barrels and pulled out a headless ax handle.

"Good-bye, squaw man." The gunfighter went for his gun.

"Hey!" Quinn called out as he flung the ax handle at Hyer's head.

Hyer cleared his holster with his pistol only to catch the ax handle right across his face. The gunfighter was knocked off his feet into the mud, his pistol flying.

Thorndyke was surprised. He expected to be shot. His weapon was only halfway out of his holster. He dropped it back into his leather. He stepped over and picked up the gunfighter's pistol.

Quinn crossed to Hyer who had blood streaming from his nose and from a cut across his forehead. Quinn picked up the ax handle.

Hyer opened his eyes and shook his head. He put his hand to his face.

"I'm bleeding! I'm bleeding!"

Thorndyke spun the cylinder on Hyer's pistol and dropped the bullets into the mud.

Thorndyke looked at Quinn.

"I owe ya '."

Quinn shrugged as if to say, it was nothing.

Thorndyke grabbed Hyer and lifted him to his feet.

"Luther," he said to Bobbs, "He got a horse?"

Luther Bobbs was near the stage. He crossed the street to a grulla hitched at the saloon.

"I'll get it."

As Bobbs stepped up to get Hyer's horse, Fenn came out on the porch of the saloon.

"Don't run him out till he pays what he owes."

"How much is that?" Thorndyke asked.

"'Bout a dollar and two bits."

"Thorndyke checked Hyer's pockets while shoving the young man through the mud. He found empty pockets. Thorndyke took the pistol and tossed it to Fenn.

"This'll have t' do."

"I'll kill you fer this," Hyer said to Thorndyke.

"Didn't you just try that?"

"Him, too," Hyer said towards Quinn. The blood was still streaming down the beaten man's face.

"Don't waste your time, son. I ain't worth killin'," Thorndyke said and then, nodding in Quinn's direction he added, "That man rode with Jeb Stuart. He can shoot the eyes out of a jack rabbit at a full gallop. You're lucky he didn't kill you."

Luther Bobbs met Thorndyke and Hyer in the

street with Hyer's horse. Thorndyke forced Hyer into the saddle and slapped the animal on the rump before Hyer could even get the bridle in his hands. The animal carried the gunfighter right out of town.

The stage driver climbed onto his seat.

"All aboard!"

Sarah had come back out and joined Quinn again. St. Clair, Guthrie and Reilly were there as well.

"Jess will see that you get home," Quinn said to his bride.

Sarah turned to St. Clair.

"That's sweet. Thank you."

"Of course," St. Clair said.

Guthrie added, "I'll go that way, too. Jest in case."

"I appreciate it," Quinn said.

He shook hands with St. Clair and Guthrie and then took Sarah in his arms for a good bye kiss.

Thorndyke came around the coach and went to get his rifle box. He looked to Quinn.

"Much obliged," the rancher said.

Quinn nodded and climbed on board the stage. Sarah blew him a kiss.

The stage pulled out and lumbered down the street in the opposite direction the Quinns had come when they arrived.

From inside the coach, Quinn looked back for one last look at Sarah.

St. Clair helped Sarah down and she sloshed through the mud to her wagon. Guthrie stood holding the horses as St. Clair helped Sarah onto the wooden seat. Guthrie tied his mount to the back of the wagon and got up beside Sarah. She gave him the reins.

St. Clair crossed over to his wagon, mounted it and followed Guthrie and Sarah down the street out of town.

Thorndyke headed for the saloon.

CHAPTER SIX

Tarr Phillips rode slowly, hunched down in the saddle, a bear of a man on a bone tired horse. The horse and rider came upon a road and turned to follow it. The horse and rider were oblivious to the passing stage which traveled in the opposite direction.

Quinn saw the figure outside his coach window. His eyes narrowed. There was something threatening about that man.

***

St. Clair helped Sarah down from the wagon at the Quinn place. It was a new house with a new barn and fences. It was a farm with hope and promise.

Ned Guthrie unhitched Sarah's horse and led him to the barn.

Sarah climbed the two steps to the front porch.

"Well, thank you, Jess — Ned, she said."

St. Clair had gotten down from his wagon to open the barn door for Ned. He waved his acknowledgment.

Ned returned to the wagon and got his horse.

Sarah stood watching when something caught her eye.

Tarr Phillips rode by as he continued toward town. He saw Sarah on the porch but nothing registered on his face. Still he continued to look at her as his horse walked on by.

Uneasy, Sarah sought the protection of the house, going inside quickly.

Guthrie looked toward the road and the rider.

Phillips was gone. But the sun was setting and evening was almost there.

⚜

The four riders, what was left of five from before, came down the muddy road. Like Phillips, these men and their mounts appeared to have come a great distance. These were hard men who were going beyond human endurance.

Inside her farm house, Sarah was looking at the wooden horse Luther Bobbs had given her. Sarah suddenly looked up as she got a chill. She bolted the front door closed and got the rifle from over the fireplace. She levered a round into the chamber. She sat it down near her rocking chair.

The four riders passed by the Quinn place without taking any note of the farm. They came and disappeared as if they were dark spirits from another world.

Thorndyke sat in a chair near the stove in the Elite Saloon, his new Winchester on the table in front of him. Fenn leaned on the bar while Shambow paced.

"I never said I couldn't do th' work," Shambow said. "I am doin' it. I'm goin' back to the shack. It's Clovis turn for a break. I'll be coverin' fer him like he done for me."

"You tellin' me you can do the work?" Thorndyke asked. "All of it? Shambow, you ain't gettin' no younger."

"Oh, hell. I still pull my share."

Thorndyke thought for a moment before he spoke again.

"Tell you what I'll do. I'll send one of the other hands out to work with Clovis. You can work with me — long as you can keep up. Get on out to th' bunkhouse."

Shambow almost broke his neck stumbling to get on his coat and out the door. He bumped into Luther Bobbs who was returning from the depot in a hurry — a little out of breath.

"You won't believe what I jest seen! " Bobbs said to Shambow but also to those inside the saloon. "Comin' this way."

"What?" Fenn asked from behind the bar.

Bobbs stepped across to the window.

"Damn! He's comin' right in here!" Shambow said.

Fenn headed for the window himself.

"Who in th' hell are you talkin' 'bout?"

"Phillips. Tarr Phillips!"

"The Ranger?"

"I seen him once in San Anton. He took on the Effelberg brothers." Bobbs said as he crossed to the stove. "Both at the same time. Kilt 'em, too." The old horse wrangler waited there expectantly.

Fenn stayed at the window.

Only Thorndyke sat back undisturbed.

From the outside heavy footsteps were heard.

After a moment, the doors banged open and there was no one standing in the frame. The only sound in the saloon was the creaking of Thorndyke's chair. He calmly rocked back and forth.

The towering man finally stepped into the doorway. His wide brimmed sombrero sagged around Phillips' heavily lined and bearded face. In his arms outside his buffalo coat he cradled a large bore .10 gauge double barrel shotgun.

CHAPTER SEVEN

Texas Ranger Tarr Phillips scanned the room with his tired but sharp eyes. He crossed the room to the back door. He pulled it open, looked out, and then closed it. He snatched a chair and crammed it under the door knob, wedging it tightly in place. Then he crossed to the window.

Fenn made way for the big man and the barkeep worked his way back behind the bar.

At the window, Phillips paused and checked out the street. He then turned to glare at Thorndyke.

Thorndyke held the Ranger's look without blinking.

Phillips took a table near the back door, furthermost from the stove. His back was against the corner. He faced the front door.

He laid his .10 gauge across the table, drew two pistols and deposited them on the table, too.

With a look he communicated to Fenn that a drink was required.

Fenn moved quickly. He took a bottle from under the bar and a clean glass to Phillips.

Phillips fished a silver dollar from his pocket, flipped it to Fenn, who almost dropped it in his haste to get away and back to the bar.

Thorndyke stood and pitched a silver dollar onto the bar.

"Fenn," the rancher said, "I'll be on my way."

Phillips eyed the remaining men only a second before he poured himself an overflowing drink which he downed in a single swallow. He went to work on the pistols. Checking each he dried them off using a handkerchief which he had produced from inside his buffalo robe.

Thorndyke exited the saloon, taking his new rifle in its box.

Phillips pulled several shotgun shells from his belt and stood them on the table in a straight line. He poured himself another drink and waited.

Luther Bobbs stood near the potbellied stove and was apprehensive. Neither he nor Fenn wanted to miss anything significant, yet there was a strong sense that they could live a lot longer if they got the hell out of there. They were torn with in-decision.

The sound of approaching horses was heard. Bobbs crossed to the window.

Phillips looked up at Bobbs.

"There's four of 'em," the old wrangler reported.

"There's gonna' be some killin' in here in about a minute," Phillips said. "You fellas might want t' get somewhere else."

Fenn and Luther exchanged looks and then did just as Phillips had suggested.

The two men from inside the saloon rushed out with their hands held up and stepped into the muddy street. They headed for the depot.

The four gunmen rode up in front of the sa-loon. They were all wearing slickers against the rain. They took them off and tied them behind their saddles.

The leader was Gus Fry, 58, ridden hard and put up wet way too many times. He had a cruel sneer, was unshaven with salt and pepper hair. He turned to the half-breed beside him.

"Round back," he said to Sam Deerinwater. The Indian was somewhere between 25 and 40. It was hard to tell. He had an emotionless face. He nodded and took his rifle with him toward the rear of the saloon.

Fry gestured toward one of the two remaining riders, Pete Guard, 43, a hard man with a mean look of a vulture about him. Fry motioned Guard toward the saloon. Next Fry looked at the Kid, maybe 16, scared but trying to hide it. The Kid was trying to learn how to be an outlaw.

"Back Sam up," Fry said

The boy took a breath and then slogged off to follow the half-breed.

While Pete Guard stood by the saloon's front door, Fry turned his horse and trotted across the street where he tied up his animal.

He pulled out his Winchester and crossed back to the other side of the Elite Saloon's front door.

CHAPTER EIGHT

Tarr Phillips heard footsteps on the boardwalk. Then they stopped. He took the shotgun shells one by one and inserted three of them between the fingers of his left hand. The one remaining shell he lodged between the second and third finger of his right hand.

Then he casually reached for his .10 gauge and aimed it toward the front door using the table to help steady the weapon.

There was a small metallic click at the back door. Phillips looked around the edge of the wall toward the rear door.

Some pressure was being applied to the door, but it was held fast by the chair. The knob turned back and then was still.

Phillips directed his attention now to the front door which opened slowly. Pete Guard, the hard vulture like man with one arm, appeared in the doorway. Phillips squeezed one trigger and his shotgun exploded.

Pete caught the blast full in the chest. He was lifted off his feet and thrown dead out onto the board walk.

The Ranger twisted in his chair, slipped his .10 gauge around, and fired at the back door. The door splintered and a man's dying scream was heard.

In a move surprisingly agile for a man of his age, Phillips bound up from his chair and lunged behind the bar where he hit the floor.

The Ranger broke open his shotgun, shook the expended shells from the breech and reloaded with two of the shells between the fingers of his left hand. The move was made with calculated ease. He had done this many times before. Then he was still, listening. There was only silence.

Phillips struggled to his knees glancing into the mirror behind the bar. He could see the open front door. Firing as he rose to his feet, he blew the Elite Saloon's lone window into the street. He rolled over the bar, fired a second covering blast at the gaping hole which had been the window, and made a running dive for the wall beside the jagged frame.

He reached inside his buffalo robe for more

shells but was stopped by the sound of running footsteps from the outside. A voice called from outside the saloon.

It was the kid. "Hey, Uncle Gus!! Wait!!!"

Phillips slung his shotgun away and dove out the window. Phillips slammed into the boards, rolling to a stop against one of the porch posts.

Gus Fry was mounting his horse across the street, leaning low in the saddle. He slapped leather while throwing wild shots back toward Phillips. The Kid rushed to his horse and clung to the saddle horn as his mount pulled free of the hitching rail and began to gallop out of town.

Phillips stood and fired both pistols — finally using the weapon in his right hand to throw three shots at Fry — but the outlaw escaped.

The Kid was in the saddle now, throwing shots toward Phillips as he tried to duplicate Fry's exit.

A chunk of wood was blown out of the post near Phillips' head.

He holstered one pistol and used both hands to steady the remaining six-shooter. He fired twice.

The young rider's horse went down, flipping the gunman headlong and screaming into the mud. The Kid's screams stopped abruptly as he smashed into the mud, his neck snapping on impact.

Phillips used his pistol again. He aimed and fired.

The body of the Kid jerked with the impact.

Then he crossed to where the Kid and the horse were sprawled in the street.

He reloaded the pistol in his hand as he stepped up and used his boot to kick the boy's body over violently.

The face of the young outlaw was spattered with mud. There was still innocence about it in death.

The Ranger had no reaction to this. He became aware of the slain gunman's wounded horse.

The beast thrashed about in unbearable pain.

Phillips softened and even shook his head a little. He raised his pistol and fired at the horse's head. The animal went still.

❧

Available at Amazon in e-book, print, and Large Print

Occurrence At Latigo

TWO FREE E-BOOKS

[Murder in Muleshoe]
If you were murdered would they try to find the killer or plan him a parade?

[Guns Along The Rio]
In 1858, two fresh-off-the-ranch 17-year-olds join the Texas Rangers. What could possibly go wrong?

GO TO: http://eepurl.com/dKEi_Y

ALSO BY THE AUTHOR

Novels

[Westerns]

Guns Along The Rio

West Of The Frio

A Hard Line Between The Rios

The Mormon Marshal

Along The Outlaw Trail

The Gavel and the Gun

13 Steps To Hell

Incident At Lajitats

Pancho's Pilot

Return to Redemption

Occurrence At Latigo

The Hussy and the Hardcase

[Political Fiction]

The Reluctant President

The Reluctant Incumbent

The Reluctant Candidate

The Elected President

[Vietnam]

Through A Lens Darkly: Vietnam

[Mysteries]

Murder In Muleshoe

Corpse In Canyon

The Lovecraft Murders

Short Stories

TALES FROM THE ALASKAN GOLD RUSH

Klondike Justice

Dangerous Camp On The Kenai

The Winds of Skagway

Screenplays

6 and 10

The 7th Luger

Afternoon Delight

Angel's Revenge

Between Love And Murder

Blood Drive

Death Scene

The Defection of Grigori Dorsky

The Evil Eye

Fatty and Hearst

Gideon: The Horse That Saved Texas

Hell In Paradise

Hollowpoint

Holiday For An Assassin

Horse Thief Hollow

Incident A tLajitas

Love, Lust, & Life

Mom & Apple Pye

Pancho's Pilot

The Prometheus Peril

The Rape of Sarah Quinn

Reservations

River of Tears

Seven Reasons Why

The Thing About Love

The Texas Rattlesnake Murders

Too Good To Be True

The Vampire Rose

A Violent End

The Virgin Casanova

Plays

Antigone In Texas

Cyrano

The Last Virgin From Las Vegas

The Seven Keys

The Unwed Widow

www.ingramcontent.com/pod-product-compliance
Lightning Source LLC
Chambersburg PA
CBHW071503170626
46811CB00007B/2714